In Concrete

Anne F. Garréta

TRANSLATED BY
Emma Ramadan

DEEP VELLUM PUBLISHING
DALLAS, TEXAS

Deep Vellum Publishing
3000 Commerce St., Dallas, Texas 75226
deepvellum.org · @deepvellum

Deep Vellum is a 501c3 nonprofit literary arts organization founded in 2013
with the mission to bring the world into conversation through literature.

FIRST EDITION, 2021

Support for this publication has been provided in part by grants from the National Endowment for the Arts, the Texas Commission on the Arts, the City of Dallas Office of Arts and Culture's ArtsActivate program, and the Moody Fund for the Arts:

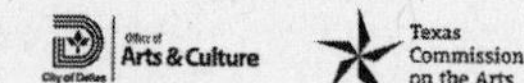

This work received support from the French Ministry of Foreign Affairs and the Cultural Services of the French Embassy in the United States through their publishing assistance program.

Cet ouvrage a bénéficié du soutien des Programmes d'aide à la publication de l'Institut français.

ISBNs: 978-1-64605-055-0 (paperback) | 978-1-64605-056-7 (ebook)

LIBRARY OF CONGRESS CATALOGING IN PUBLICATION DATA

Names: Garréta, Anne, author. | Ramadan, Emma, translator.
Title: In concrete / Anne F. Garréta ; translated by Emma Ramadan.
Other titles: Dans l'beton. English
Description: First edition. | Dallas, Texas : Deep Vellum Publishing, 2020.
| Originally published in French as Dans l'beton by Grasset in Paris, France in 2017.
Identifiers: LCCN 2020044985 (print) | LCCN 2020044986 (ebook) | ISBN 9781646050550 (trade paperback) | ISBN 9781646050567 (ebook)
Classification: LCC PQ2667.A7737 D3613 2020 (print) | LCC PQ2667.A7737 (ebook) | DDC 843/.914--dc23
LC record available at https://lccn.loc.gov/2020044985
LC ebook record available at https://lccn.loc.gov/2020044986

Cover Design by Marina Drukman

Cover photograph by Jan Helgason/Alamy.com

Interior Layout and Typesetting by KGT

PRINTED IN THE UNITED STATES OF AMERICA

IN CONCRETE

ALSO BY ANNE F. GARRÉTA

Sphinx

Not One Day

To Emmanuèle Bernheim

Missing you

IN CONCRETE

1.

Short the Suffering

CONCRETE'S NO JOB FOR SISSIES.

Maybe that's why our father decided, soon as we were old enough, my little sis and I, to educate us in cement, concrete, and casing.

You could sorta say, thanks to our precocious education, that my little sis fell into concrete as a young girl. Sorta.

For you to understand concrete, I'd have to explain an infinite number of things. I'd really have to get myself together. And I'd have to begin.

I'd have to.

But where to start? The end? The beginning? The middle?

And where is the middle, anyway?

In shit, there's no middle. There's just shit. Shit's the milieu . . . In concrete, it's the same.

So may swell begin at the beginning.

I have to tell you, then, that my little sis and I poured our first concrete in very remote times, still-primitive times. We did it by hand. As in, with a shovel. It was before our mother gave my little sis, our father, and me a concrete mixer. It was for his birthday, but it was a present for us, too.

A red concrete mixer with a 2-HP electric motor.

It changed our lives. It muddernized us. We started working on big projects with our father on an industrial scale. We'd concrete every weekend in the countryside, even some of summer vacation too. Every time we drove to town for groceries, our father would say, coming out of the butcher's, for example:

"How 'bout we go grab a bag of cement next door?"

My little sis never said no. Our mother said nothing. (I never had a say.)

I also have to explain, so you don't misinterpret my mother's silence, that concrete, lime, cement, mortar, hybrid or not, with or without a mixer, is awfully messy work. Our mother wanted to keep us clean, even on the weekend. That was the rule. So there were endless loads of laundry, big ones. So many loads and so much mess that the washing machine couldn't take it anymore.

Our father had a theory. Those machines have weak innards. They're not designed to guzzle so much cement and gravel. They're not concrete mixers. Though in theory, a concrete mixer and a washing machine work the same. But ingesting all that muck was like gulping down fatty food that turns into pipe-hardening cholesterol, or stones in the urethra. The machine guzzles, chokes, then flocculates and coagulates. The drain stops working, the guts clog. And then bam! Infarction, ictus, and splosive diarrhea.

At night in our room when we went to bed, my little sis, who'd spent an entire laundry cycle feeling up the machine and listening to the sounds of its insides, confirmed the diagnosis. It's like when you have a stomachache. The machine gurgles, hiccups, or worse, and then makes a ghastly effort to empty its guts out one end or the other.

I wondered if the machine was suffering, if it wasn't cruel to make it keep choking our laundry down.

But whether spunky or sick, it was clear that it no longer met our housekeeping needs.

The dirty laundry kept piling up. Our mother was losing all hope of keeping us clean. She and Grandma polished us from top to bottom, morning, noon and night. But the Portland would bind with the sweat, the rain, the hose's excretions. We were ashen. We shed spalls into our soup. The made-in-France natural boar bristles clothes brush no longer sufficed.

Our grandma switched to a wire brush.

And then we'd come back all plastered after a

session with the concrete mixer, and she'd have to work her fingers to the bone again to deplaster us with her poor primitive methods.

One day, at lunch, watching us shed lumps into the grated Gruyère, our mother threw the brush into our father's noodles and started to cry into her own.

Our father needed things explained. How the boar bristles brush worked, and the wire brush. The reason for its sudden appearance in his noodles. I couldn't do it, my throat was in a knot just seeing our mother salting her noodles with her tears.

Total bewilderment.

In such cases, my little sis is the one who comes to the rescue. Little sis is no sissy, you see. Quite the opposite. Bewilderment? She spits on it. The bewildered? Pansies and pussies. They enrage her. She reviles them, big time.

Insults like that motivate the bewildered. They snap back to life.

As for our father, it galvanizes him, even.

He said all the machine needed was a simple triple bypass. I open it, I dismantle it. I brush the filter vigorously, give the ducts a good sweep. I change the pump . . . I have an old one saved up that's like new. I cut a piece of the garden hose . . . it's long, there's plenty. I tighten the clamps, fit the sheet metal back on. I put the whole thing back together and it's good as gold.

Since the noodles had gotten cold after so much bewilderment, and were too salty even before our mother had cried all over them, we began the operation without delay.

We assisted our father.

He felt it was important to teach us, to demonstrate things. He's always loved to pontificate. To wax and buff philosophical, too, sometimes, and intrepidly. But mostly to give orders.

He's a leader and a pontiff.

Leader, pontiff, sure, but pedagogue, never. That's a bad word, a suspect word, a word that stinks of tearooms.

What tearooms? And what do tearooms have to do with our training? And how many cups of tea does it take to be able to profess and wax and boof?

We don't know, and he won't say.

A riddle wrapped in a mystery inside an enema.

The bypass, in any event, was an opportunity to pontificate. Later in life, whenever we were thrown a curveball, it came in handsy, all that waxing and buffing and all that polished pontification. You can't count on repairmen, all they do is tell you your machine, that one there, it's fucked and you gotta buy a new one. You don't say! They take their customers for chumps. Often, they're not wrong.

We followed orders. We brought our father the tools

per the necessities of the operation. We held the flashlight so he could see the failing organs he was hunched over. We set aside the bits of entrails he handed to us over the course of the dissection. In our pockets we stockpiled the little screws, the little joints, the teensy nuts and bolts, those itsy-bitsy things that are easy to lose and then later you find yourself up shit 'crete.

We were learning new vocabulary, all the technical terms of the trade: bitch, crescent wench, o-ring, cotter pin, a pox on your house, hex driver, piece of shit, sleeve clamp, and go fuck yourself!

When it was over and we'd de-poxed, re-erected, taptaptapped, and butted and plugged everything, he said, Let's test this bitch.

And into the drum he shoved all our rags, stiff with cement.

Often, there were leaks. Our father called them incidental leaks, collateral leaks, even. They tended to intensify. According to my little sis's calculations, the volume of the incidental drainage rapidly approached that of the nominal drainage. The laundry room turned swampy.

I have to explain one thing: this was before we decided to lay in a concrete floor like you might've seen in a Jerry bunker. Cause before, in primitive times, before we really radically muddernized, the laundry room floor—which used to be, in more ancestral times, possibly even prehistoric times, a henhouse—its floor, before the Teutonic slab and muddernity, was a dirt floor.

Hens the swamp.

Hens the stagnation and the unexpected humidity that rusted the sides of the bitch, specially where our father whacked it with his hammer to put it back together after its open-heart surgery.

Hens the laundry, waiting to be washed or freshly cleaned, spilling directly into the sludge. Which was bad news for the machine's bowels.

Hens the sighs of our poor little mother whom our father forbade to do the laundry without her boots on. OD green rubber boots, which we'd given her specially for her birthday and for the laundry room.

It wasn't so much the sludge that my father was worried about. Detergent, cement, and bleach by the glassful to top it all off, that'll kill the bacteria, guaranteed. The soapy, caustic mud wasn't much of a concern. The lack of electrical insulation, on the other hand . . .

The lack of electrical insulation scared us. All the more so since in those ancient times, you have to understand that our electrical setup was also primitive. We had demonstrable proof. In fact, we were reminded of it every day.

For example, we used to have a nice wood-burning stove, with iron cabriole legs. Louis XV-style. This stove did it all: cooking, hot water, heat. But, electrical everything! That was the muddern mantra. So we chucked the wood-burning stove, and our father replaced it with an electric range. When you turn on the oven, the circuit overloads, the breakers go snap! poof! It's simple, our father explained to Grandma, when you want to use the oven, just unplug the fridge and it won't fry the fuses anymore.

Often, by the end of summer vacation, after so many tripped circuit breakers, we didn't have any fuses left. So we boiled water for coffee with the help of a blowtorch.

But the worst was the lamps.

Our father doesn't like waste. He repairs things with old recycled wire. The cables get shorter. The lamps in the house give us a shock every time we try to turn them on. We don't dare touch them anymore. We're like rats in a lab experiment. We'd rather stay in the dark and wait for someone else to sacrifice themselves, resign themselves to getting electrifried for the common good.

I'm getting a bit sidetracked with these electrical deviations (but not smuch as all that: everything is connected, this is a serious web I'm tangled up in), a bit derailed from our original affair—the story of the concrete.

So, to recap: the concrete mixer was suffering,

the washing machine was suffering, our mother was suffering.

My little sis pointed this out to our father with great tact and composure. And as soon as he was good and bewildered, she insulted him BIG TIME. There was nothing he could do but take the matter to heart and, pronto, by the horns.

We had to short the suffering immediately.

2.

Grind the Past

ONE WEEKEND, BARELY OUT OF the car, our father went straight to the henhouse-laundry-swamp, grabbed the machine in a clinch, and laid it down sideways on the recently soaked ancestral dirt floor. A one, a two, a three, we lifted it up: our father on the motor side (where it's heaviest), my little sis and I on the other side (she on the right, me on the left). And we pulled and pushed, dragged and dropped it on the grass in the courtyard where it puked up what was left of the bile and gravel in its guts.

It stayed there for a good month. Several weekends, I remember. Grass grew around it while we were busy muddernizing the swamp, wading for the delivery of the brand-new machine our mother had ordered for her own birthday.

It was all sorts of muddern. You wouldn't believe

our laundry room had ever been a henhouse. A concrete slab, reinforced with rebar, that I'd floated perfectly and in total bewilderment under the stern direction of my little sis, who'd taken it upon herself to motivate me vigorously. Spanking new PVC drainpipes. Plumb and level wiring running in Schedule 40 conduit. And even waterproof junction boxes, which we diswaded our father from improving so they wouldn't be totally shot before we'd even used them.

We got extremely filthy, our father, little sis, and I, while laboring to short the suffering of both our mother and our washing machine. So filthy that we were able to inaugurate the new muddern laundry room in splendid fashion. After our mother, Grandma, and Grandpa inspected the installation and little sis explained to them the technical advantages, the three of us stripped down to our underwear, loaded the machine, and then, bare feet nice and dry on my slab, we watched the drum turn through the porthole all the way until the final spin.

The old machine was still lying on the grass outside. Don't think for a second we had kissed it goodbye.

First, we had to salvage the laundry we'd forgotten inside the day our father moved it. It'd gotten a little moldy. Our father discreetly exfiltrated the spongiform, fungusy chancroid—that's what he called it—to the far end of the garden so our mother would be spared any bewilderment. He said that with a bit of bleach and a lot of sun, it'd turn out fine. But it was a rainy summer. We had to use a shitload of bleach on it and our mother suspected something was afoot, even if she didn't say anything.

Next, the washing machine. You didn't really think we'd trash it at some garbage dump, did you? That's not our style, not in this family. We don't just throw things away.

Especially not machines.

First off, it's too cruel: you don't just ditch a machine you've lived with, spent hours disemboweling, repairing, insulting, a machine that's provided you with so much filth and cleanliness, so much muddernity and anxiety. And it's preslicely because the machine is old and sick that you can't abandon it.

You'd suffer too much.

And you never know: it might come in handsy.

If there's a war, if the Germans come back and loot and mow us down again along with our resources, our young recruits, our electrical appliances, our Jews, and our muddern thingamajigs, we'll still have our old machines, our junk, our scraps, our incidental leaks, and all the rest. Our father, back to the soil, will plow with a Citroën DS engine mounted on a lawnmower towing a plowshare that Grandpa will bequeef to us from his old farming days. That's how we'll grow potatoes. We'll hide people in our laundry room. Our mother will be able to do the laundry in the backup concrete mixer to keep us clean. We'll want for nothing.

So, no, we don't trash our junk, we don't even retire it. We're like the French army with its elderly generals: we send them to the reserves.

For our reserve corps, our father requisitioned the barn. That's where we stash all our rustbuckets, our fubar machines, our broken tools, all the scrap iron, the incidental waste and collateral damage of our muddernizations. Rusting peacefully, in the cool and the shade. Like in a museum or a hospice or an academy.

It's not a cemetery, don't go believing that. Well, maybe. If you're a true believer, maybe you could call it a cemetery. Our father is a believer. He puts his faith, strong as stainless steel, in the resurrection of machines, junk, scrap.

Very early in life, he told us . . .

I mean very early in his life, but also very early in sis's life and mine, when he said it . . .

Shit.

Here I go again, getting all tangled up in the barbed wire of time . . .

Lemme start over: very early in life, his and ours, he told us that he felt an inclination to care for all those paralytic rattletraps, aphonic radios, and frenetic washing machines. He wanted to save them. And he never stopped, he never gave up, not even when faced with cases that seemed mechanically, humanly, and electrically hopeless.

The concrete mixer is a living example of our father's vocation.

I have to mention something very important regarding our management of the reserve corps and also our family's faith, which is that our machines wear out quickly—more quickly, obviously, than they would in the hands of wusses. Since refurbishing, fine- and refine-tuning, and ball-fiddling is not our father's style.

We realized pretty quickly, my little sis and I, that the concrete mixer, robust as it was, would give out on us and bite the rust one of these days, like all the rest, like the lawnmower, the washing machine, the drill, the chainsaw, and so on and so fork.

My little sis diagnosed the ailment. It started out like Parkinson's or mad cow disease. When the concrete mixer concreted, it would go all spastic, its welded steel legs shaking and rattling, its gear teeth chattering. My little sis climbed up on my shoulders to examine it one morning after our father had gone into town to replenish our Portland supply.

I'll summarize the etiology of the illness and its course, as elucidated by Poulette that very night in our bed.

I'm getting ahead of myself again.

First I have to explain why my little sis's nickname is Poulette, and why we shared a bed.

So.

It's not that we didn't have enough furniture. But in the still-ancient times I'm talking about, she would often invite me to sleep in her bed. I thought at first that it was because I meant something to her and that she loved me, in a way.

Later, when we'd finished muddernizing from the ground up and we had central heating in the house, she stopped inviting me. When I asked why, she gave me a reason so rational I couldn't hold it against her, sad as it made me.

Poulette was sensitive to the cold, because she had very long legs, which are an asset in certain situations. For example, they give her a fearsome reach on the field or when kicking balls. But from a thermal point of view, they're not very efficient: by the time blood arrives to her distant extremities, it's already cooled off. If she'd been squat, like me, she would never have been cold.

So, it was mutually beneficial, a rational division of labor according to our innate advantages: I benefited from her long limbs, she benefited from my caloric efficiency.

Now that part of the story's been nailed down.

At least, half nailed.

I'll hammer home the rest later. But even half nailed, things generally hold together pretty well. That's what our father says anyway. There's wiggle room, he says, there's redundancy; we leave that for the finishing touches. Often, he's not wrong. Things vibrate, wobble, lean, withstand gravity by the skin of their teeth, but we still have some doors, some shelves, and some pipes that haven't collapsed.

I'll bet it's the same for you.

Back to the pathology, lickety-split.

My father, who was always in a rush to finish and so hated the finishing touches, the fine-tunings, the pussyfooting, the wussyboofing, and the finitude of all things, our father would often neglect to rinse the mixer thoroughly after it was done serving up its concrete. Meaning: incidental residues would get stuck in the cogs' teeth. Next time around, the poor thing would rattle as it chewed, ground, and rechewed, between pinion and crowned wheel, the gravels of yestergear and the remnants of slabs past.

From all that crushing rumination of the past, it'd start to rattle and wheeze. That's what wore out the heart of our concrete mixer. Until the fatal day the engine shuffled off its mortar coil.

That happened the exact same day little sis fell into concrete, so to speak.

But I have to clarify so's to avoid any misunderstanding or slanderous insinuation.

First off, I have to make clear that the concrete mixer really suffered that day.

Next, what happened to my little sis is not the concrete mixer's fault at all. It's no one's fault. Or if anything is to blame, the only thing we can blame is time.

Yeah—it's time's fault.

It was that very day, and on that very occasion, that I understood something crucial, something of which I had no inkling previously: I understood that, as those English sissies say, it's all a bladder of time.

3.

All a Bladder of Time

THERE'S NO SHORTAGE OF GAS. Along with the reserves housing the widgets and whatsits, out in the country, we also have a strategic reserve. Just like the Yankees. Who're no sissies. We've seen all the John Wayne westerns with our father: Yankees are no Englishmen.

We pile up jerricans and demijohns in the old rabbit hutches. We've got everything we need for two-stroke engines, four-stroke engines, even diesels. We can power lawnmowers, rustbuckets, and, one day when we're rich, a generator. You never know.

And in fact, it does come in handsy. It's not a useless precaution. Because even without wars and embargoes, we've run out of gas. Often.

Our father's penchant for experimental science has a lot to do with it.

For example, on trips to the countryside, he likes

to test the capacity of our bladders and the rustbucket's gas tank, simultaneously. Who can hold out the longest without pissing; how many miles can we drive with the gauge on the dashboard in the red. Sometimes we wind up full to burst and on empty, simultaneously. It can't be voided.

Hens the usefulness of the strategic reserve, and also the very belated muddernization of the shitters. When nature calls—I mean, when it *really* calls—who needs a bathroom, a bowl, and a flush, huh?

The methodical beauty of the simultaneous experiment on our bladders and on the gas tank, especially when we're far from our strategic reserve, and in spite of our mother's pleas--she wants us to stop at the next gas station—No, no, you'll see, I bet we can make it till the next next one—the beauty, I was saying, of the experimental method, is that when we finally run out of gas, we're thrilled to stop and finally piss. We're broken down and we're relieved.

Who keeps hanging her head in despair? Our mother.

The best part, as our father taught us: all you have to do is piss in the car's tank and then you can get going again.

No shit.

Our father demonstrated this experiment for our mother very early on, even before she'd become our mother (it was on their honeymoon, apparently). And he redemonstrates it regularly as needed. Because a need (for fuel or for a piss) shouldn't go to waste: it's a golden opportunity to apply the experimental method and to pontificate.

The theory, confirmed by our repeated experiments, is as follows.

Primo: even when the gauge says the gas tank is empty, there's always a little left. All the way at the bottom. Unclear how much, but never none.

Secundo: a combustion engine can function perfectly without any serious issue using gas that's been slightly diluted, or even comfortably diluted. It emits a little water vapor, that's all.

Tertio: it doesn't wreck the engine.

Quarto: even if it wrecks the engine, all you gotta do is repair it.

Conclusion: with a full bladder and a theoretically empty tank, there's always a nonzero chance of reaching the next service station. In case of emergency, just pee in a hurry and remedy the shortage with urine.

I call this the peenury theory.

It's all a bladder of time, I said. The proof is that when we hold in our piss for two hundred miles, time passes slowly; and when we've pissed into the tank and we have to get to the next service station, time races by, not even three minutes in and our mother starts to panic.

It's an observation I've made often and reflect on at night, when it's calm, when there's no one to bewilder me or hurl insults at me.

When we can't piss, time doesn't piss either. When we've pissed, time seems to gush. I don't have any experiential proof, but it seems to me that, from a certain perspective, it's as if time, real time, is not what you see on watches and clocks. And that real time, in fact, trickles. So, if God exists, he must be a prostatic and incontinent old man, and the universe is his bladder.

Or his chamber pot.

In any case, the end of time will look like a big old chaotic colonic.

Seen from that angle, life's but a tinkle, isn't it? Caesar or Victor, I can't remember which, wasn't being fuelish when he said, I came, I saw, I squatted. *Punto basta*.

What's any of this got to do with concrete?

Tough nut to crack. The day I figured it out, it felt like an epiphany. An intuition, as my grandma says. But later, it became obscure, murky, despite the nights I spent trying to make it into a theory that would hold up.

You need the whole story to see the relation between gas, guts, concrete, and time.

Here we go.

Our mother had inherited a farm. A real dump. Remote, not far from our country place. An old uncle who'd kicked the bucket and voided his bladder once and for all.

We drove there after the estate lawyer notified us.

The horror! The horror! Worse than our house premuddernization. No running water, just a well. There was electrical power, but only in the barn. Earthen floors that hadn't been rammed since we last thrashed the Krauts, and not just in the henhouse: everywhere. Zilch by way of concrete, modern comfort, or laundry room.

Our mother was at a loss for what to do with such a liability. Uninhabitable, unsellable, unrentable.

We put her on the train back to Paris. She had to get back to work. Otherwise who would provide us with our concrete mixers, our washing machines, our generators? We stayed in the countryside with our father and Grandpa and Grandma.

We were on our way back from the train station when our father decided to surprise our mother. We would muddernize the hovel, we'd do it quick and dirty. One or two slabs of concrete, but lightweight concrete, you hear! A mix of chopped straw, gravel, and Portland for example. A chouia of electricity, just a bit of plumbing, and it'd be a dream little farmhouse in the sticks for a Parisian or even a Brit who's not too queer. Calm, bucolic, and muddern at the same time.

So we threw ourselves into this new muddernization. Our father had calculated that this big project would take a week. Then we'd see about the finishing touches.

Let me skip the details and concentrate on the concrete.

Our father's bright idea was to convert the attic. We would pour a slab on the upper floor, instantly doubling the square footage and thus the value of the hovel. That's where we had to start. In a single day, the three of us would concrete it. It wasn't a dick for sissies, but seeing as we weren't sissies, it was no problem.

First, before we could even level and nail the expansion joints, we needed a clean underlayment. So we had to chuck out the residue, the ancient debris, the heaps of waste left behind by mice who'd snarfed up the leftover seeds that used to be stored up there. And then beneath it all, another rammed earth floor.

My little sis and I crushed it up with a pickax. Our father shoveled it all, dirt and waste, out the dormer windows.

We started to suffocate almost immediately.

To keep our lungs from filling with ancient dust and vermin effluent, our father had swaddled our muzzles in rags. We looked like Mexican bandits waiting to attack the stagecoach in a John Wayne western. But it got hot. We were sweating. The dust stuck to the sweat on our foreheads and dripped into our eyes.

We had to cry in order to see.

We were desiccating fast. The bottle of water our grandma had given us didn't last long, even though our father sacrificed his ration for us. That's what a leader, a pontificator, has to do: sacrifice for his troops.

He cheered us on, C'mon, one more little square foot, over there, by the wall. He set the example, he gave the commands. But very quickly his throat got too dry, even for pontificating. We shriveled silently, to the whistling of our lungs and the clearing of our throats. But hard on we held. Only sissies capitulate. Hard on we held, focusing on the beautiful slab we were going to pour. A tough task too, but less dusty.

And then there was a mishap . . .

4.

Ballseye

YUP, A MISHAP.

The fully loaded shovel that our father went to chuck out the dormer window blew right back in his face: the bran, the dirt, the mouse droppings, all the ancient muck blasted back by a gust of wind. Straight into his eyes. Our pater was blinded instantly.

And not a single drop of water left. And no running water. And no pump yet, which we were supposed to connect the next day, and not even a bucket to take to the well. Nothing. Zilch.

He bellowed, Aye! Aye! Aye! Fuck! I can't even rub my Eye! Eye! Eye! Kids . . . ! Help me! Where are you? C'mere.

We drop our pickaxes and rush over.

He looked like an albino rabbit rolled in flour, our father, so fast was his eye pinkening.

We suggested jump-starting his lachrymal glands. But he needed to tell us how. Cause we'd never seen him cry in our entire lives. Even when he missed the nail and slammed a hammer on his fingers—which happened often. Even when he rolled over his riding lawnmower into stinging nettles, brambles, or barbed wire. Or when he scorched himself welding. We'd never seen him cry. So we didn't know how to go about it.

How could we make him cry?

A little pickax strike on the corns of his feet?

That would leave him stoic. He wouldn't even bat an Eye! Eye! Eye!

I could tell my little sis would've liked to suggest a swift kick to his privates but was afraid it would bewilder him. And then she'd have to hurl insults at him. Which was hardly decent for a man—or even a rabbit—in such ocular distress.

He had a better idea. There was no more water, okay. There was no water. But there was a solution. In fact there was exactly one solution, and we had to act fast. He demanded it. Under normal circumstances, such things aren't done, but M'eye! M'eye! M'eye! He was hurting so badly . . . That muck sanding his corneas was truly disgusting.

So there you have it.

We would spit.

We absolutely had to.

We had to spit on him.

Point-blank.

It was an order.

In his face.

Cause there was really nothing else to do in those extreme circumstances. So, hop to it, lickety-spit. But not just anyhow, anywhere. We had to take aim. We had to spit right into his eye. Saliva, nothing but saliva. At our age, we hadn't yet had time to catch any sort of nasty clap. And by the way, saliva isn't even that dirty, it even kills certain bacteria. He'd explain this to us later. Gotta spit, plain and simple, and fast, cause Oye! Oye! Oye! Holy fucking shit, he was going to lose his Oyes!

Little sis didn't hesitate for a second. She tore off her bandit rag. She planted herself in shooting stance and started to muster all her ammo for a first salvo.

Our father knelt for the execution. At our level, so we wouldn't have to aim too high. There, just right, straight ahead . . . Line of sight, ballistic trajectory, she couldn't miss.

Knowing Poulette, I expected a top-notch bloogie.

But it was pathetic, a pitiful little nothing, not even spittle: three splutters, two drops, worthless.

Poulette didn't go soft. She dug deep, deep as she could.

I tried to do the same. I thought that if I really loved our father, I should be able to summon a little something.

But I had nothing, nothing in the tank, nothing at all. It was the Sahara.

My little sis, who's more affectionate than I am—so says our father—my little sis, whatever she could scrape, whatever she could muster, she spat point-blank into his reddened and shit-beset eye, which gratefully welcomed her little green and greasy gob of spit.

It wasn't enough though. We needed more. And better.

We could see our father was suffering. But we couldn't salivate any more than we could cry, no more than he could. We were on empty after all the dust and sweat. None of our useful glands were functioning. The lachrymals? Arid. The salivaries? In arrears. We didn't even have to piss. Total peenury. These were desperate times.

I had no saliva, but I had an ingenious idea: I asked Poulette if she was hungry.

Oh, she was hungry.

So I told her to think of all the things she wanted to eat, her favorite dishes. To really focus on them. Intensely. To imagine them in her head, smell them, even chew them. A meal fit for a feast, like Grandma cooks for us. With loads of desserts. And not just desserts. All the mashed potatoes her little heart desired, if it came to that.

I started up the same film in my head. First I

thought of a chilled vichyssoise. With little asparagus tips bobbing on the surface. I concentrated on the broth and I felt it coming. To sustain the trickle of drool that was forming, I helped myself to a tartine of chopped liver. I dipped it in the soup. Now I was getting somewhere: I was able to launch a humongous sticky spurt straight into our father's left eye.

Poulette was in charge of the right eye.

After the tartine, I ordered blood sausage with apples on a bed of little croutons rolled in butter. That did the trick: I mustered up two clear liquidy loogies that glanded smack in the paternal eyeball.

Ballseye! I yelled to egg us on.

Our little albino rabbit let out a sigh of relief.

Once little sis and I had unblocked our glands, it was easy as pie. We scarfed down everything we could think of and belched galore. There was no stopping us. Salvos of saliva. Sizable geysers. We even stepped back to see who could spit the farthest. We tried to outpace each other. Right, left, right, right, left, right, left, left, left. Optimal parabolas like we'd learned from our field artillery instruction manual, then lobs just for spits and giggles. We could've rinsed off our father's entire mug without losing steam, we were cooking with gas. We had the strategic reserve and our glands working at full capacity.

I hadn't even gotten to the cheese course yet—I

was already dreaming about a petit-suisse with quince jelly on top—when our father cried uncle.

We pleaded, Just a little more, snot clean enough, it's still dirty, there's still some in the corner of your eye, don't move, we'll fix you up in a jiffy.

But our father isn't the type to linger on finishing touches. He stood up. He wiped the drool streaming down his face with his bandit rag. And as soon as he was dry, he grabbed the butt of his shovel and dug into the whole heap of shit anew—but making sure, this time, to keep clear of the blowback.

And we lingered there, Poulette and I, filled with all that affection, all that accumulating saliva we didn't know what to do with since our father no longer wanted us to spit on him.

We were foaming at the mouth.

So we spat in each other's faces.

Reciprocally.

We announced the dishes ahead of each strike. Frisée salad with lardons, incoming! An order of nice blue Roquefort, coming right up!

Poulette didn't play fair: there were as many greasy gobs as clear loogies in her dispatches. We finished dessert: a chestnut cream crème fraîche, square on the nose, a raspberry sorbet straight to the forehead. We even exchanged cordials right to the face. I shot chocolate truffles that narrowly missed her as she dodged, while her marzipan bites dripped into my ear.

We were beat.

We couldn't take it anymore.

All that food without anything to drink, and in that heat.

We felt a twinge of indigestion.

Once the heap of shit was out of the way, we cleared out. Talk about a big day. We'd saved the paternal eyeballs. Heroically. Thanks to us, he wouldn't turn into a blind rabbit with a white cane.

We've had many similar on-site adventures, zeroic ones, and on that construction site they even happened every day, as you'll see if I ever reach the end of this damn concrete story. But this particular adventure, and this particular day, were exceptions to the drool.

Cause that was, after all, the day I learned that there are times when spitting in the face of our elders is a matter of filial duty.

A duty to all mankind, even.

5.

Buffed to the Core

So it turns out there are times when spitting in the face of paternal power is a filial duty.

But apparently you can't brag about it, because in the car on the way back from the site, our father made us promise to keep it a secret.

So, as you can see, concrete is full of lessons, even if I can't spell them all out at once. But there will be others, there will be others, just you wait. It will all be hammered home in the fuelness of time.

Concrete also creates lasting memories.

For example.

Since that day, every time I see a western and there's a Mexican bandit with a rag over his face, well, my salivary glands get all excited. On the one hand, it's not unpleasant, cause it reminds me of how we saved our father from going blind. But on the other hand, it's embarrassing to drool so much, especially in public, and without being able to explain to people how or why, since it's a secret.

It also happens to me in front of people with pinkeye, or people who've cried a lot. When I see their red eyes, compassion overwhelms me and I start to salivate. It scares people. They think I'm about to bite them or have an epileptic fit. They are of course seizurelously mistaken about my intentions. Often, it pains me to witness such total incomprehension, and it makes me want to cry, but then they might think I'm a pansy and I'll have no choice but to fly into a rage. So I don't cry. I suck it all back in, saliva and sobs.

Another annoying memory nestled in my glands is the blood sausage with apples served alongside little croutons rolled in butter. The sight of them on my plate, or even just on a restaurant menu, brings tears to my eyes. Not cause I'm sad. I adore blood sausage with apples and the sweet little croutons, all nice and fried. But that dish gets my lachrymals flowing, nothing I can do to stop it. What's bizarre is that asparagus tips don't have the same effect on me, not chopped liver either.

What gets to my little sis is mashed potatoes. Since we have them more often at our house than blood sausage with apples, which is a dish my grandma saves for special occasions, little sis gushes over her plate more frequently than I do. It saddens our grandma, who can't understand why her grandchild is dripping tears into the mashed potatoes she so adores. You can tell because she always asks for more and then cries anew over each plate.

Since we can't explain it, cause we've been sworn to secrecy, we've tried lying, saying it's because she loves mashed potatoes too much, and because I love the little croutons, and that we're crying tears of gratitude. But no one believes us. And our father, with each serving of mashed potatoes, has to lower his eyes to his plate to avoid Poulette's tears and to hide his own bewilderment. (He doesn't care for blood sausage with apples, so Grandma doesn't make it when he's around.)

I've pondered this over many a night.

Yeah, at night.

There's a secret I haven't yet dared to tell, but it's time.

It's a tricky confession, trickier than you can imagine.

But I have to, so that you understand, and so the things I still have to set in concrete aren't so obscure.

It's a goddamn tricky confession. So tricky, it's twisting my insides.

You can't repeat it.

You can't repeat it, but in my head, at night, I wax and buff.

When Poulette falls asleep on her tablets, that is on her koala (I'll explain all that later . . .), I'm no longer afraid of anything.

So I wax and buff.

I concrete in my head, or I run wires, or make up stories and theories. And I wax and buff. I really focus. I do everything spit-and-span, spanking clean, steady and methodical, always beginning at the beginning. Slabs smooth and level. Theories about intuitions. Impeccable trowelings. Experimental mental science. Leak-proof pipe couplings. Zero collateral damage. And when it goes to shit, I start over. Make it even better. With total aplumb. Checked with a spirit level. Set straight.

And I wax and I boof.

So much so that in my head, I worry I'm a certified fairy.

But it's like my lachrymal glands when I see blood sausage with apples, or my salivary glands when I see rabbit eyes. In my head, when it's night and everyone's asleep, my brain can't help itself from buffing down to the core.

All this concrete in my head, all this brain juice leads to unfortunate consequences that I can't keep secret and can't secrete.

For example, it takes me hours.

So getting me up in the morning is mighty bewildering.

A real bullfight to get me up, my father and Poulette say.

I'm the bull.

If my grandma hadn't been around to save me, I would've been at death's drawer a long time ago, no grout about it.

Anyway. It's a grief I know will hound me; we'll talk about it again later.

One night, I couldn't hold back, between buffing a couple of concrete slabs in my mind, from thinking again about that whole gland thing, and how strangely it works. I read in a book once that we have little glands all over our bodies, and that they're useful for loads of things. Basically, as far as animals go, humans are pretty damn glanded.

I wondered if all these glands we have everywhere, unbeknownst to us except when they don't work and we need them to, or when they've taken a beating and become glandicapped, I wondered if it was possible to motivate them, like when we salivate thinking of things that delight them (like blood sausage with apples) or that pain them (like a father who's been glandsformed by a blast of air into a giant albino rabbit).

And then I also wondered whether it wasn't there, in the glands, that our memories reside, and even whether they can travel from gland to gland, like the mashed potatoes that migrated from my little sis's salivaries to her lachrymals.

Of course, not all memories gland up there. Only the ones that manage to escape from our brains, which are real prisons.

Another unfortunate consequence of all the nightly glandemonium: I keep imagining all our construction sites, our father's and my sis's and mine, and buffing them ahead of time.

I anticipate, I rehearse, I polish.

I adjust the expansion joints with the spirit level, I rake and tamp down the bed of pebbles before starting up the concrete mixer and dosing the aggregate.

It's worse with wiring. I run verticals and then horizontals for hours in my head before installing all the junction or wall boxes. I measure and remeasure before pulling the wires through the conduits; three per circuit, a red one, a blue one, and a yellow-green one. I wind colored tape round each end so's not to confuse the circuits, like our father did in the laundry room. Three complete circuits per 25-gauge flexible insulating duct.

I screw around and I buff. Too much time on my glands.

And then Poulette and our father scold me later on the job.

I do it all in my head, and they needle me, they jostle me.

You gotta hustle, you gotta make it happen, even if it mishappens.

If there's a mishap, we'll repair it later, when we're on the finishing touches. We're not here to stir-fry the slab with sweet little scallions. We'll still be here tomorrow at this rate. You gotta move on, we're not taking root here.

Get a move on, gofer it! They're gofers, my father and sis.

I worry like a sissy cause the joints are all lopsided, and when I try to be exact, I end up pussyfooting even though I'm no pussy. I lose hope cause we eyeball everything, and then, later, the concrete pulverizes and cracks, and all the crap from everywhere seeps into it and it's as though there were no slab and all our hard work was for diddly snot. And then I crack cause when there's no more red, our father just shoves two yellow-green wires into the circuits, which is exactly how we wind up with an electrical fault that will one day end up killing our poor little mother.

Our father couldn't give a hoot about electrical faults and shorts. He's used to them. He's vaccinated against them. He gives himself booster shots all the time. We hear him yelling, Fucking fuck! and Fuck shit!

Everything goes on the fritz.

Our mother faints.

We aren't bothered: we know it's just our father who's electrifried himself once again.

Even when ostensibly it's not the electricity he's

fiddling with, our father still finds unexpected ways to shock himself. He can electrotoot himself with absolutely anything, that's how ingenious he is.

With a circular saw, for example . . . all he has to do is cut into the cord at the same time as the board, and bingo: Fuck, double fuck, and goddamn!

He can even do it with the pump that pumps the water out of the well. For that, he just has to have neglected to fix it solidly. It hangs by the electrical cord, which is a piece of crap, not at all sturdy, it frays all the time. When we've fished out the pump from the bottom of the well, when we've rewired it in a hurry and really fucked the screw terminal blocks with our rush job, here comes the fault. Guaranteed. All you have to do is try to restart the pump: Fuck, double fuck, and go schlong yourself!

That's why I screw around at night.

I spend more and more time in my head fixing it all, going over the places where things got fucked up, where things electrotooted and eggsploded, where things corroded, fell apart, collapsed.

I sink into melancholia.

I get bogged down in buffing and glandulation.

I get up later and later. And upon waking I discover more and more disasters and destruction that I hadn't anticipated, that I'm too late to stop and that it's not even worth refine-tuning.

Nothing ever happens the way I envision it in my head.

Cause of the mishaps.

I can't foresee everything. I can't foresee the diabolical fuckups our father invents at every turn. The unexpected collateral damages he concocts every day. I can't anticipate all the delays, the goofs and derailments that happen cause of the rush jobs.

The muddernization of our mother's hovel, for example . . . I thought I'd rehearsed everything in my head: I'd ironed out the pouring of each layer of the slab.

All ironed out, so I thought . . .

Go schlong yourself.

6.

Hoist Head

THE DAY AFTER OUR FATHER'S eye incident, we had to get down to business with the concrete.

We'd brought the pump to draw water from the well and wet our mortar. And some other knickknacks, as you'll see.

We'd loaded the concrete mixer into the trunk of the car. Our father'd dragged it up to the rear of the old rustbucket. Then, swiftly, he'd grabbed hold of it by the legs and tipped it over, drum first.

We also had several bags of cement in the front seat.

That's all you need to know to understand why the shock absorbers of our car never recovered.

They're not the only ones.

We were faced with a technical problem. The concrete mixer would sit in the courtyard of the hovel. We were pouring the slab upstairs. The concrete in the concrete mixer either needed to go up or we had to bring it up. We cut out a header in the floor to pass it through, but we didn't have a proper pump. We could scale up a ladder to the upper floor and lift the sauce in a bucket, but that'd take too long. At that rate we'd still be there when we were old enough to catch our first clap.

So our father cobbled together a solution: we'd practice economies of scale.

In our reserve corps, we had a hoist. A superhoist in a semifunctional state, guaranteed to lift up to three tons. We also had a washboiler. An ancient thing predating the washing machine era. Like a big trash can made of galvanized steel. Heavy-duty. Except it was missing a handle.

Our father came up with the idea of attaching the hoist guaranteed to lift three tons to one of the roof beams and positioning the washboiler on a nice thick scrap of white oak mounted on salvaged wheels and drilled at the four corners. He threaded wires through the four holes—four wires per hole—which he twisted tight and used to secure the washboiler, with enough extra wire to form two handles on top that crossed at a right angle, and to which he fastened the hoist's load chain and lifting hook.

I feel like you need a drawing to really grasp these two handles. But don't look at me. In my head, I draw perfectly well. But only in my head. You'll have to take it up with the koala . . .

Right, the koala . . . I'll get back to the koala later, right now I don't have time: we're about to board . . .

Our father calculated everything in theory. The weight of the concrete—light but not too light. The wire's elastic resistance to twisting and loading. He had Poulette double-check all the additions and multiplications. And now he's ready to prove to us that it's solid. He's already tested the system, but we're going to retest it.

Empirically and in situ, he says.

We're all three of us going to climb into the washboiler. We're going to pull on the chain, which'll activate the hoist. Us three weigh just a little less, in theory, than half a washboiler of concrete. A half washboiler, that's our unit of measurement. He promised: we won't weigh it down any more than that, we'll keep some wiggle room.

So we board the washboiler. We hoist, empirically, the part of the chain that activates the ascent in situ. Slowly at first, to absorb the slack, and then, when there's no more slack, rather brusquely. The wheels leave the earthen floor, the washboiler lifts off, and us three in the basket rise.

It holds very well, this hoist is no piece of crap, it's definitely solid. We could even hop up and down or swing back and forth. Our father encourages us.

We hop up and down for a good while in the wash-boiler moored at attic floor level. Okay, the hoist is up to the task, we've proved it.

Empirically and in situ.

We can go back to earth.

Our father grabs the other length of chain, the one for lowering the load. He pulls on it.

Nothing happens.

He hangs from it with all his weight.

Nothing: the hoist is completely unmoved by his request.

Maybe it's just a kink in the chain.

Our father tries a hanging-hopping-swinging maneuver to unblock it.

Still nothing.

We're starting to get pretty antsy inside the wash-boiler. Ballooning gets boring, especially empirically. It gets old real quick. Still the same beaten earth floor that hasn't been beaten since we were clobbered by the great Fritz offensive in Artois. Apparently after that, we couldn't beat anything anymore, not the Fritz, not the dirt. Beat around the bush, maybe . . . And even then only in our heads . . .

But now I'm the one beating around the bush . . . talking about Artois and offensives while we're still stuck up high in situ while the hoist . . .

Our father has a hypothesis: it must be one of

those adamant aggregates of an old concrete that's jerked itself into the chain, jamming up the pawl. He says we have to do what we do when one of the rust-bucket's wheels gets stuck in the mud: a little nudging motion back and forth, to regain traction. Regaining traction is one of many ways we help him, my little sis and I, whenever the family gets stuck in a rut, usually as soon as our mother's a little distracted. So, the idea of a gentle alternating nudge back and forth seems reasonable to us.

So let's see if it comes unstuck when we ratchet up a notch or two and then quickly yank in the other direction.

The problem with this damned hoist that doesn't want to gear into reverse is that with a notch here, a notch there, then another little nudge, our traction's like a tablet of chocolate being nibbled: soon there's no more. We ascended several yards, we used up the whole chain, and now we find ourselves face-to-face with the beams.

Which is paradoxically not so bad, cause our father is finally ready for his close-up with the hoist head.

Fortunately, to add weight, we brought along a sledgehammer. So our father can give the hoist a good smack, BLAM!, and then another, REBLAM!, on the other cheek—to balance it out. But the hoist head is unconvinced, and the chain remains kinky. We do another round, right-left, BLAM! and REBLAM! on the gearbox.

No go.

We're not going to spend the day in a washboiler twenty feet off the ground, clobbering like chumps at a fucking hoist head that doesn't want to budge. It's painful, this mishap, and concrete can't wait.

At the eleventh hour—which is upon us: we can't get down and we can't ascend any higher either—in this kind of situation, with no way out, you gotta do what you gotta do. If we have to lower ourselves, we'll lower ourselves.

We'll even shtoop to pussyfooting.

We'll sneak attack it, we'll sweet-talk it, that bitch of a hoist head: we're gonna grease you up, gonna lube you down, gonna buff you to the bone.

Our father will hop out and go search down below for what we need.

Meanwhile, little sis and I will stay put.

Except we almost toppled out of the washboiler when our father hopped over the side and hung from the chain. It pitched abruptly. I held on to my little sis, who held on to me. In a pickle like this you can't go soft and say every man for himself. That's how disasters happen.

Our mother often tells us, in a family you have to stick together. She also says, nothing can ever get between Poulette and me.

Sure enough that's what saved us from going overboard. We formed a bonded pair, a compact block that wouldn't fall through the handles of our washboiler. Thanks to which we didn't spill out and splash onto the beaten earth twenty feet below like two little selfish heartless shits.

It went swimmingly.

Except that in the aborted disaster, we lost the sledgehammer.

7.

Going Soft

Except that in the narrowly aborted disaster, we'd lost the sledgehammer, the fucking sledgehammer that didn't have the presence of mind to cling on to us.

It took a dive and hit the ground at the same time as our father, who'd slid rapidly all the way down the hoist chain. So rapidly that the chain got hot and sanded all the calluses off his palms and maybe even a little more than the calluses.

So, sledgehammer and father landed at the same time. In fact, the sledgehammer landed on the corn on the little toe of his right foot.

But, since we heard nothing—nothing at all: no fuck, no shit, no sonofabitch—we didn't suspect anything. Bizarrely, he didn't suspect anything either. Between the concrete, which was becoming urgent, and the kinky hoist, suspicions were a luxury. We were focused. We forgot to feel.

It wasn't until later, much later, that we realized the sledgehammer, upon landing, had ampootated our father's toe.

Clean off.

But ampootated or electrotooted, our father, in the heat of the moment, in the urgency of the concrete, wasn't thinking about his giblets. It's always afterwards, always later, when we have time to twiddle our thumbs, when things aren't urgent anymore, that we hurt.

It's leisure that makes things frantic. It's time that hurts. Nothing else.

And indeed we didn't have any time toulouse, and our father soon came back equipped with everything he needed to anoint the hoist.

Sliding under our car, he had bled a chouia of oil from the engine, just a chouia! He had collected it in a slightly rusted can commandeered from the ruins of an ancient pigsty.

All Poulette and I had to do was lift up this providential oil, being very careful not to spill it, by pulling on the chain, attached to our improvised vessel by a bit of barbed wire that'd been spirited from a nearby fence.

Precision, fluidity, dexterity. And above all no abrupt movements. We did our best, Poulette and I, and once we held the holy vessel in our hands, having managed to unhook it from the chain, our father climbed up the chain to join us in the washboiler and bless the hoist head like a real pontiff, with some good emollient grease and a few swings of the censer while Poulette and I tolled the bells by pulling on the chains and singing at the top of our lungs DING! DANG! DONG!

With patience, with oil, with DLING! DRANG! SCHLONG!, and BLAMS and REBLAMS, the hoist finally loosened up.

Hallelujah! we chimed, Poulette and I.

Our father, to speed along movement, celebration, and concrete, gracefully parachuted overboard once again. He hung from the chain, now running marvelously, and as a result landed on the dirt floor at optimal speed, knees bent, thighs ready to spring into action like the certified parashtupist he really is, badge, wings and all.

And we too, raring to go and thrilled by the lubed swiftness, sprung knees taut from our washboiler at the preslice moment when it collided KABOOM! with the dirt floor and we roly-polied nimbly thereover.

Not a scratch!

The 2nd Foreign Parachute Regiment couldn't have done any better.

It's all about practice. Being chuted or electropooted, it's all the same. You gotta have training, reflexes, alertness. Cause if you take the time to contemplate, if you think about what you're doing and how, well then either you're dead or you end up not doing it.

Which amounts to the same.

Cause when you're dead, you don't do anything anymore.

And if you don't do anything, how do you know you're not dead?

Our father assures us this skilled chuting of his has saved his life and even his balls more than once.

Once upon a time, however, it almost killed our little mother who was peacefully reading the newspaper in her room after lunch, lying on her bed.

Don't worry, I'm not going off on another tangent. I'm not drifting.

This ties in neatly with the concrete.

It wouldn't have happened, in fact, if we'd poured a good concrete upstairs. Or if we hadn't run into a mishap installing the floor.

I also have to admit that in this particular attic, there wasn't much light. And our father was making his way in the dark, loaded up like an ox with a big bag of plaster mix, or maybe two, or even three or four (to get the job done faster). And to get them onsite from the strategic stockpile, he had to walk through the darkness, on a rafter or maybe on a board spanning two rafters, because of the delay in laying the floor.

It's wild, the mishaps we experience with our father.

We're quite intimate with mishaps. We rub shoulders with them every day!

In return, the mishaps may simply rub us out sooner or later.

Just like our mother, who nearly fell victim that afternoon while reading her paper.

So.

So, in the darkness, staggering from one rafter to another weighed down by his load, our father made an unfortunate swerve, a teeny-weeny swerve, a swerve only half the width of a rafter, nothing at all, a pittance . . . but that pittance sent him over the edge, up the creek, basically dragged him into total enterocolitis: feet together on the light latticework supporting the ceilings of the rooms below.

And I remind you, in case you lost sight of her, that my mother was in one of those rooms, calmly reading her newspaper, as I said, not imagining that the sky could, in her own home, on her own bed, one calm August afternoon, fall on her head even though we weren't at war, neither civil nor uncivil, and there weren't even any pacification ops going on that she was aware of.

But the sky, but the plaster, but our father.

Feet together on the latticework, yup.

Perhaps if he'd gently set his foot down, just set

it down, nothing would've happened, maybe, just one foot, just one . . . Maybe the latticework could have held.

But weighted down as he was under his bags of plaster mix, our father couldn't hang on to anything.

And just like that, down he went, smashing through the lattice, crumbling the ceiling, dropping through the plaster nearly onto our mother frozen with terror, who doesn't have the reflexes to get out of the way when the mishap came crashing down on her in the form of a sweaty, plastered, splintered man finely lacerated by fragments of lattice, chutist and rubble fallen from the heavens in a single torrent of dust, bran, and mouse droppings.

Mishaps aren't something you get used to. Gotta train yourself.

Our mother lacked such rigorous training.

Every time disaster strikes, our father swears it won't happen again, that it was purely an accident, and our mother believes him, trusts him, lulled by assurances that never come to pass.

Little sis and I run our own bootcamp: we crawl through mud and cow shit, we roly-poly under barbed wire, we mount assaults on hay barns and practice chuting from the tops of haystacks. We're training for the next war, the penultimate war, the one after that and even the next next one, in case we find ourselves back in the days of the Battle of the Marne, the Nivelle Offensive, D-Day, and Sainte-Mère-Église.

We steal sheets from the armoires to fashion our sails, a fashioning that requires a lot of knots, mostly knots, even exclusively knots, and very tight ones (which later plunges Grandma into despair).

We stealthily steal into the neighboring barns on recon ops. We hoist ourselves up hay bale cliffs and then, deploying our bags of knots, we jump.

But the cushiest jumps, I'm telling you, and the most rare, destined for imminent extinction, are to be found on the farms of the old peasants, the stubborn old-timers: where parallelepipedal bales of straw form splendid staircases, where hay heaped high higgle-dy-piggledy on the lofts offers landings deep as tombs and fragrant as Grandma's armoires.

But I digress. I dip into reminiscences, drunk from so many free falls. I devise delicious mortal mishaps for myself, and the story is as stalled as the concrete.

At this rate, we'll be here until the cows come roam, until pigs cry.

But that's cause there's no one to help me. I have to do everything in this story: psychology, descriptions, soldering, electricity, concrete. And keep it grounded or else we end up electrifried. Pull from this bag of knots the wires that belong to the proper circuits and not bollix the breaker box. Avert the short-circuits, the lack of insulation, the insufficient amperage, and the voltage drops. Not mix up phase and neutral.

Make no mistake: when I concentrate, I have proper syntax and even spelling. But when there's too mush rushing around and I have to tell it all in one go, it's too mush pressure, it bursts out of me, and then my gramma suffers.

She's the one who keeps us clean when our mother's absent. She also scrubs our brains with spelling and sums.

I'm hounded by remorse.

I don't like to make my grandma suffer, but Poulette and the pater reproach me! They muck up everything . . . the concrete's making no progress, it might even be receding . . . and the story isn't faring any better. Mishaps and setbacks mar all our sites cause we're always shaking a peg! Then it's my gramma who suffers, I can't even spare her my hasty grammar, my syncopes and apocopes, my horrible apheresis and other crazy crases.

And there's no one to hold a light for me when I'm in the dark.

And then there's the bladder of time. Writing is urgent. Like concrete.

It must go on.

So as soon as we landed on the dirt floor, Poulette, our father, and me, we launched our mission. Our plan of attack:

I was upstairs, ready to receive the washboilers.

Poulette was below, working the hoist to send them up to me.

Our father was in the courtyard, in charge of the concrete mixer and the loading.

He shoved in the granulates, then the cement, and when the aggregate was nice and blended he added in mixing water from the pump. We told him to follow the proper sequence of operations. It's slower than doing everything all at the same time, but there's no comparison when it comes to the finished product. Nice and smooth, just how the blend should be.

Poulette inspected the load before hoisting. She was inflexible with regard to the levels. She didn't hesitate to send back a washboiler that was clearly overfilled.

Finally, she'd hoist, and I'd lean fearlessly over the joists to grab the one handle and give the washboiler a little swing once it reached me. Without vertigo and without fear, I emphasize, cause to prevent any untimely falls we'd fashioned me a solid harness out of rope, a real chutist's harness, except with no chute, just tied to a chain fastened to the wall. Long enough so I could reach the edge and not a hair farther.

So I would lean without fear, gauging the amplitude, the period of oscillation of our concrete swing, and I would rock the washboiler hard as I yelled to Poulette, Slack!

This was the critical moment.

At the exact second Poulette, unhoisting at full throttle, dropped the washboiler, I had to pull it to me by its only handle so it would land smoothly on the floor.

When I say it like that, it sounds easy. But first off, syncing slack and swing is an art. Next, you can't even imagine how heavy concrete is.

A little washboiler of concrete, of lightweight concrete, just a little washboiler, and, again, only half full—it's heavy, lemme tell you. Swinging it back and forth is exhausting. You have no idea how, oh how exhausting, all that concrete!

Even so, our father loaded and unloaded the drum. Poulette hoisted. I swung, she dropped. I rocked and yanked. I rolled, I spread, I raked. No going soft. Later we'd all trowel together.

We'd been slogging away for two hours when there was a mishap.

The most serious mishap we'd ever had.

It was worse than Berezina.

Agincourt, Thermopylae, we could've saved face.

Waterloo, Dien Bien Phu, the Dardanelles, we would've known what to do, thanks to all our training.

But this, this was the scat's pajamas of scatastrophes. What we saw unfurl was essentially the end of days, the end of all setbacks and blowbacks. A free fall feetfirst into the apocalypse . . . into the fatal shitpit, if you like, which is to say into concrete.

All cause we'd gone soft.

8.

Monstrous Scatastrophe

YOU WANT TO HEAR ABOUT the disaster that befell me on the edge of that joist where my chain was keeping me.

Though the memory makes my blood run cold with terror, I'll oblige.

I will scribe on the tablets the story of that monstrous scatastrophe.

Here we go.

It was as though . . . Careful! I said as though, not ass though or as dough, which would make no sense at all . . . It was as though a tremor shook the place, even more than a tremor, more than an explosion, more like a colossal toppling of everything—period. The walls teetered—semicolon; as though the hovel were pulling off of its foundations to prance about—line break.

Springing from the washboiler that abruptly

dropped like a bomb—comma, KABOOM!!! a towering tawdry column headed straight for me. Yup, tawdry—new paragraph.

Of all the trees, pine trees bear the strongest formal resemblance to this phenomenon—colon: a longissimo trunk that flares into a dense crown, spotted and lurid in some places. I said lurid—Lima Uniform Romeo India Delta—period.

But no new paragraph!

Too late . . .

Already the branches collapsing under their own weight fall down—semi-colon; straw lumps and gravel coated with blue-green mortar lambaste the floor—and an ellipsis . . . And no helmet, no pillow to protect my head

we were still in the early hours of a long summer eve and yet an uncertain, languishing light was spread over everything

the gray greasy horrible creepy goop papers the walls blankets the dirt floor it blurs

Poulette

the washboiler

the oak scrap

unfortunate phrase when you think about it

oak

scrap

the sooty darkness thickened

I raised my hands to the sky and convinced myself there was no more hoist no more washboiler no more wheels or oak scrap and that this concrete was the last

the final concrete that would bury
Poulette
ground
scrap
dump
world
me
and all hope of muddernization
amidst such pitiful peril I didn't voice a
complaint a cry
I didn't fall into
unconsciousness
or a jeremiad
or any sissy business
a chimera
deplorable and dumb
founding at the same time
sustained me
All the universe
was sinking
with us
into
the
sea

ring

gray

ness

You're slipping! You're slacking off! Such anarchic proliferation of paragraphs is not civic at all. And those little strands of lines that vermicelli the blank surface of the mental page . . . You're nibbling tablets in your head, and when the whole thing is all gone, what will we do then?

And what about the punkchewation, huh!? You're chucking punkchewation out the window?

Get a hold of yourself, Fignole! Bunker down! If the entire universe were to sink with us into the searing grayness, down to the last comma, I would still have to scribble it all down preslicely on our tablets.

And, as for the searing grayness—comma, it was everywhere. Make sure to scribble that down. The fulminating eruption, the lapidary geyser, the splosive scatastrophe, the concrete volcano had obliterated everything.

If the washboiler was Vesuvius then the hovel was Pompeii, with Poulette buried underneath.

I see the light anew, even the ground, pale and smoky as during an eclipse. I see the disaster at my feet that has blanketed everything and, like a statue, the mute form of Angélique draped in mortar, crystallized in a pearled concrete syrup, smothered in brutal gray.

Lucky, they say, are those to whom the favor of the gods—or if not the favor of the gods then paternal klutziness—grants the privilege of experiencing things that deserve to be scribed!

Lucky also, it seems, are those who are entrusted to scribe on the tablets the things that deserve to be recorded, such as paternal klutziness and lapidary scatastrophes!

And even luckier are those, like Poulette and me, who are given the double privilege of finding themselves encased in greasy mortar and feeding the koalas.

Yup, the koalas . . .

Don't ask me why koalas . . . Can't you see it snot a good time?!

As for klutziness, if you don't know what that is, let's just say to keep it short that it's the specialty of generals, of top brass and rulers. But snot just them. Klutziness worms its way into everything. No need to be a high roller to be swimming in it. Klutziness has no end, no limit, and it's within the reach of any ol' poodle.

Epic klutziness, imperial klutziness, the lurid panache of klutziness pushed to heroic apogee and even to entropic scatastrophe—I fear we're the last of the klutzes.

Lucky! Quoth the optimists . . .

Have they never scribed on tablets, those bearded clams? Have they never taken a geyser of fresh concrete to the kisser?

Angélique! I cried, Angélique! and I yelled, pulling on my harness like a dog on its leash.

My little sis, Poulette, is named Angélique.

Yup, Angélique.

I'm up a creek.

First it's koalas . . . then it's klutziness . . . and now it's Poulette. While all around us lurk imminent danger and monstrous scatastrophe . . .

Angélique!

And I can't fly to her rescue! Cause there's no way to unhook my chain, and no way to chute from the joist to go eggzoom my little sis. Cause even though I yell Angélique! Angélique!, our father, busy with his drum of straw-concrete, can't hear a thing over all the squeaking and squawking of the concrete mixer.

Since in any event I can't do anything beslides yell, and since even that is worth zilch, I might as well settle my debts and tell you the origin of the nickname Poulette.

THE STORY OF THE CHICKEN AND THE CHICK

Before our little chick Poulette became Poulette, she was Angélique. That's her real name, the one she takes to school. But in the countryside, she happened to form a rather unique friendship with a chicken in the neighboring barnyard. An authentic black hen that was eggzeptionally nice, a humanist hen who, as soon as she saw my little sis arrive on her bike in the barnyard, rather than scramming and clucking, considered her with a round but curious and not at all fearful eye.

Upon seeing which Poulette, who was not yet our little chick and who still answered eggsclusively to the name Angélique, got off her bike, grabbed the black hen, shoved her under her arm, and swoop! kidnapped her with a kick of her pedals.

That's how it happened.

Why did the black hen put her trust in my little sis, who was quite capable of slitting her throat and chucking her back among the terrorized polychrome poultry with a pulsing red geyser where her mohawk should've been?

This hen's immediate affinity for Angélique, hensforth our little chick magnet, is a mystery that can't be explained.

For, in the end, how do we know whom to trust?

We've all known geese, turkeys, chickens, even rabbits who believed the farmer who fed them every day was their best friend (or even, in fact, their mother). And then when they finally understand the sad truth, they rush to seek shelter at the butcher's . . .

Possible that the black hen was astute, a real genius. Perhaps she reasoned thusly:

1. In any case, I'm clucked;

2. Between the farmer, the fox, the butcher, and the kid, I have to take a gamble;

3. So let's go for the kid on the bike. Ride or die. It's time! This place is boring. Let's set sail. Raise anchor! Cast off! Even if I lose my head, might as well see the world.

That's how she became Angélique's hen. And Angélique, reciprocally, became the hen's poulette. She brings her sidechick with her everywhere; they're inseparable. Koala on her back, hen under arm, one hand on the handlebar, and off to the rodeo (more about the rodeo later, later . . . you'll see . . .).

That saved the young black hen from the chopping block.

Or perhaps the young rooster . . .

Who's to say? It's not so straightforbird . . . When it comes to poultry, you can't just go groping their butts . . .

But I'm getting off topic.

And what's the koala have to do with any of this?

9.

Way Way Out in the Sticks

I KNOW, I PROMISED YOU the koala ages ago. But the koala'll just have to wait. Cause Angélique candied in her mortar is turning into a concrete-crusted Poulette, and rescuing her is urgent. Now here comes our father to fetch the washboiler for another round, only to discover the disaster.

We were up the concreek again. In the soup, the pâté, the pudding . . .

Call it what you like . . . the schmear, the guts, the schmuck, the silage, the dysentery, the cecum, the horror, the Turkish delight . . . I'm at a loss, I don't even have the technical vocabulary to describe such distress.

Our father immediately sized up the situation, took aggressive measures.

Civilian imbeciles would've lost their heads and

rushed round the ostensible victim, namely Poulette, disregarding the basic principles of triage.

Not our father. The doctrine is clear. Inflexible. We stick to it.

FIRST, unchain me.

Then, and only then, dysenter Poulette.

Was she breathing? Was she wounded, was she shot? Was she in shock? Bleeding? Conscious? Was anything broken?

We palpate her, we move her. Nothing dislocated. We're reassured. We congratulate her. And her skull, how does Poulette's skull feel under her bunkerskin skullcap?

Had to disinfect and inspect her.

We'd never have enough saliva, and even if we pissed on her . . . let snot go there. So we turn to the filbert, to the trowel, the Flemish trowel, even the joint trowel.

The finishes are infinite.

We've sacrificed all our bandit rags, but she's so drippy that nothing's working. The more we trowel, the more we scrape up that cement snot, the more our Angélique is slathered in it and the more we lather it when we come into contact with her, the more we sink into the slime and the more we're sucked into the muck ourselves.

Not how Hercules went about it with Augeas, I note.

So we run to pull the hose from the pump and bring it up to the rat's nest. We're about to hose Poulette down when CLACK! SHABAM! WOOP!

The concrete mixer shorts.

Massive, enormous silence. Everything tripped: the concrete mixer, the hand lamp, the pump . . .

If you think little things like this'll throw us into a panic, you're mistaken. That it'll drive us to surrender, or force us into a retreat, even a tactical one, that we'll bend over in the face of such a shitstorm and abandon the battlefield, you're farting up the wrong tree.

Fuses, we needed fuses. But of course we didn't have any in reserve. That would've been too easy. That would've risked atrophying our native ingenuity, our solid koalifications. We use authentic lead wire in our fuses. It pairs well with the ancient porcelain cutouts and the conductors sheathed in Bakelite paper. When we've finished melting all our calibrated wire, we'll cannibalize the power tool cords or the concrete mixer.

While Poulette is crusting over, while our father is tinkering around the electric meter in the barn, and while he's cannibalizing, short-circuiting, and electro-tooting himself over and over (which is old news by now and stopped amusing us forever ago), I can finally settle my debts and tell you the story of the tablets and the koala.

I promised, and I have nothing better to do.

So, while I hold Angélique's hand and as the mortar increasingly welds our phalanges together, I can pull your leg with the story of her koala. That'll weld us.

THE STORY OF THE KOALA

Angélique typically manages our accounting. The gas, the reserve corps, the countryside arsenal, the ammo, it's all scribed on her tablets . . .

The tablets are little spiral notebooks. Grandpa always gives her multiple notebooks for her birthday and also for Christmas. When there's a shortage, he loans her one from his personal stash. And he inscribes the first page, always, in ink. Clean. Neat. Admirable.

Poulette has plenty scribed on her tablets. She takes them with her everywhere packed inside the koala strapped to her back. She takes the koala to bed with her. She keeps it padlocked. She can only sleep on top of her tablets. It's a sandwich: koala, tablets, little sis.

There's plenty in there, even if I don't really know what. The contents are secret, in theory.

But when we want to know for example how many washing machine drums there are in the reserve corps, or how many electric motors we have and whether they're a little broken or a lot broken, there's no need to go to the barn, which is such a dump anyway that we can never find anything unless we crisscross the whole mess methodically. When we want to know, before attempting to go up that creek, we ask Poulette.

For example, a quasi-functioning motor, rated for 1,500–2,000 watts.

Poulette consults the koala. She pulls it out from under the quilt. She enters the padlock's secret combination. She takes out the right notebook. She pores over her tablets, and that's that.

She's the only one who can tell us how many busted drills we have in stock, how many bits of scrap iron of whatever length and however bent.

I also know she has an entire assortment of very useful charts. In addition to the multiplication tables and the logarithmic tables, she has formulas for different applications of concrete: proportions, granulometry, recommended additives, volumetric masses. She has loads of comprehensive inventories, technical vocabulary lists, plus a catalogue of all the books she and I possess jointly. I often see her copying things from the books into her tablets.

Just in case.

It wasn't our father or our mother who taught her. Our parents are chaotic as can be.

Our grandparents are very meticulous. So I think it's our father's influence that made our mother lose her sense of order. Or else she gave up and embraced his chaos out of love. It's a thing: our parents are chaotic like other couples are alcoholic. Out of love. They keep each other company in their confusion.

It's our grandpa who inculcated in Angélique the love and method for bookkeeping, the tidy sums, the little notebooks kept in perfect condition, the railroad timetables, the piggybank records, and also how to neatly tie up packages.

Angélique wants to emulate our grandpa in every way.

For eggzample.

Grandpa puts on his hat, it's time to sit down at the table. So Angélique got him to bequeef her one of his hats, and now she wears it at the table too. Since it's too big, and since it has a tendency to slide down her face, she assumes a particular posture in front of the plate: back completely straight, koala hanging from her shoulders, head steady, hat tipped back.

When we stop in restaurants for lunch on our way home from vacation, we're a spectacle. Poulette and Grandpa chewing opposite each other, very dignified in their fedoras. Our father bareheaded reading the newspaper. And then our mother, Grandma, and me chatting at the end of the table.

For now, Poulette is content with her koala, which also serves as the stuffed animal she takes to bed when she sleeps. But she's always coveted the little suitcase where our grandfather keeps his own tablets. She asked him to bequeef it to her in his will.

Without her, without him, and without the koala, we would have sunken into entropy by now.

What's entropy?

Entropy goes hand in hand with klutziness, like the chicken and the egg and vice versa. Like Moses and Pharaoh's daughter. Like syphilis and parish priests. Like manna and the desert.

What else?

Entropy is the quagmire of empire, when you can no longer escape, empirically and in situ.

Entropy is simple, says Poulette: entropy is our father.

We'd need Maxwell's demons, says Poulette, who's clever but often enigmatic.

I don't have a koala. I keep everything in my head. As for Maxwell's demons, I don't know where you'd find one, they're probably as hard to find as a noodle in a haystack. And that day, the day of the concrete eruption, we would've needed a whole squadron of Maxwell's demons.

We didn't even have a fuse!

Anyway, forget the fuses: from all the shoddy cannibal jobs and the badly calibrated wire, our father—no doubt sick of short-circuiting over and over—began to flirt with high voltage. He stopped blowing fuses: he actually melted a cable and fried the meter.

Adonai what to add.

Adonai what to subtract either.

We'd arrived at the end of the operation, the gritty, gray, dull mass of the cement layer. We were paddling up the choleric carious creek. We were up to our noses in it.

Noses, I said, not Moses, cause there was no Moses or Maxwell to get us out of this one.

It'll take more than that to discourage our father. Make no mistake. We'll rinse Poulette, pump or no pump. My harness and chain are up to the task. All we have to do is tie her up and leave her to soak in the well.

Now I can't help myself from imagining the well, the chains, the black water, the cold that whips your face when you lean over the edge even in the middle of the afternoon even in the middle of summer, the fleeting reflection of the sky turning to ink.

Angélique is imagining it too. I see her silent tears welling up from the concrete.

"Why, O why, Papa, do you want to drown our Angélique?"

Let's put her in the washboiler then! let's lift her up! hoist her! get her clean!

But the diameter of the washboiler exceeds that of the well. And the hoist! It's more than kinked now, it's plain twinked beyond repair.

We flounder and ponder, pulling Poulette inside the washboiler. Here a yank, there a yank, everywhere a yank yank—towards the well, towards the barn, and yonder through the hovel, while the greasy coulis turns to gangue and the concrete crust encasing Poulette turns into a sarcophagus.

Angélique, who was crystallized in the cement, is now rigidly encased in it. There would be no way to bend her into a seated position, even if we wanted to. If she wanted to blow her nose, she'd have to beg for help.

Little sis isn't raging, she isn't even reviling. She's too stunned.

In the waning light, our father studies Poulette planted in her zinc pot. He declares that the situation, far from worsening, as we might think at first glands, allows for remarkable tactical opportunities. He calls for the sledgehammer. He's going to unmold our Poulette . . .

Where is that damn hammer?

I protest once again.

"Why, Papa, O why would you want to clobber our Angélique?"

And with a sledgehammer! We'd make an omelet of Poulette before we managed to crack her out of her shell.

In any event, the sledgehammer is nowhere to be found. Who knows where it went . . . Drowned in the mudslide, probably, buried under the dripping tide.

At this point we'd need shears, wire cutters, maybe even the angle grinder, our pater concludes. And the box of electrical stuff. And then water and clean clothes and maybe a comb. We can't show our faces like this. Disgraceful . . .

"Children, don't move, I'll be back."

And he gets in the car. Pedal to the metal.

Through the blown-out windows of the hovel, I see the red taillights grow distant, diminish, and go out like two embers amidst the ashes of the fading day.

"Why, O why is our father abandoning us?" I ask the statue of Angélique, who sniffles meekly but still doesn't protest.

The light dims. It dims slowly. It's one of the longest days of the year, but inexorably it dims. It's evening, nightfall, dusk goes on and on, but finally it's night, we're here, Angélique and I, in the dark, in the hovel exposed to the winds, way way out in the Styx, up to our eyes in squalid concrete.

10.

Shit Creek

DON'T MOVE, CHILDREN, I'LL BE back.

We weren't going to make fools of ourselves whining like wusses, begging him to take us with him. We weren't going to follow him and eat the dust in his wake hoping he'd pick us up as hitchhikers.

We too have our dignity.

Besides, Angélique was less and less able to move or run. Her petrification was progressing at an alarming rate. Stick-straight, more and more rigid, stuck in the washboiler.

I, for my part, was standing in the layer of concrete spread over the earthen floor that hasn't been beaten since you know when. I wanted to go watch at the window for anything coming. I couldn't extricate myself. My shoes had sunk into the concrete.

Which wasn't smoothed over at all, I have to

specify, but looked more like a formless slab, not troweled in the slightest.

If I want to move, I have to undo my laces and pull myself up by my bootstraps. But even then I can't really move. Concrete, spread and dried, entraps me, forms a shell around me, and when I struggle to extract myself I feel like a shrimp, a little gray shrimp.

It makes me chuckle when I think about it, which is not unwelcome, in our situation.

And when I laugh—Ree! Rah! it cracks my exoskeleton a bit . . . CRICK! CRACK! . . .

Allow me to introduce myself, CRICK! CRACK! . . . Fignole, the little shrimp . . . CRICK! CRACK! . . . Rah! Rah! . . . CRICK! . . . Ree!

Fignole, that's my nickname.

Fignole, Finiole, or Fignol.

Like Guignol and his band.

Not a bad nickname for someone who likes to finagle. It's a little tease that even skitters sometimes into Feignole. Somewhere between feign and mole, or a fig casserole, or a finicky gloriole—careful, I said gloriole, not glory hole. The name's not Fagnole.

The worst is when they call me Fanghole. Beware teeth down there!

Poulette's fate is nobler, and her posture intrinsically more dignified. She's like Tutankhamun, a mummy, or a melted reactor in Chernobyl. In her sarcophagus she's absolutely boiling, even if we smell nothing, hear nothing, only her breathing, regular, cavernous.

The terrible thing with Angélique, as with atomic power, is that for a while everything goes swimmingly, perfect bliss, and then suddenly things fly out of control, veer into hypercritical condition . . .

What's for sure is that in a sarcophagus like this one, there's no risk of anyone munching on the munchkin, putting the mummy in their tummy, or fiddling with the atomic fondue.

Me, I could be gnawed by predatory teeth, delectable as I am, which scares me, though I try to keep mum.

I stand next to the washboiler in the darkest darkness. From time to time I taptap against the concrete veil that conceals my Angélique, CRICK! CRACK! KNOCK KNOCK! Anyone home?

I so wish she'd answer me, so wish she'd ask, Who's there?

I'd tell her, Poulette, it's me! CRICK! CRACK! Fignole, your little shrimp!

She'd say, Woohoo! Pull on the little dowel, hooray! And the little bomb'll drop, whee!

And we'd laugh—CRICK! . . . CRACK!—at our predicament.

But Poulette doesn't say a word, it's like she's sleeping, and I worry because the windowpanes are long gone, and the door of our cabin is lying unhinged on the threshold where it served as a washboiler ramp, and the night is growing darker and darker.

Time thickens like the darkness. It gets viscous like a sugar syrup or a setting blackberry jam. Then, finally, frozen stiff.

I wouldn't go so farts to say I'm on the verge of terror, but it's eerie.

I don't know if this has ever happened to you, finding yourself knock-knocking in the depth of night on the sarcophagus of a mute mummified munchkin, in a cabin with no door, no shutters, no light, and no Grandma, but it's eerie.

You hear the croaks of insects, rustlings, grinding of teeth. It's monstrous how much you can hear. Like the night is wriggling, tossing in its bed of pastures and hedges. Sometimes you even feel a breath, a gust of cold air on your face, like a caress.

And then the moon poked its head through the nearest window and the night turned blue.

I'd been feverishly praying for that moon. It was finally in the sky, and now I wished it weren't.

Who'd've thought I'd prefer the pitch dark.

At first you think pitch-black night is the worst. You want to be delivered from the darkness that oppresses you. Then you realize that this moonlight, even with a full moon, especially with a full moon, on a night with no clouds, is worse than the thickest, most opaque darkness.

Because of the fantastic silhouettes of all things in the moonlight. Because of the shadows. Suddenly the shadows that rustle and breathe.

I should start a fire. That'll dissipate the frightful phantasmagoria reigning over this armpit of the world.

Grandma told us that her own grandpa made fires at night to keep the wolves away.

When he was a child, he watched over the herds in the woods near here.

Suddenly I think of that extremely ancient ancestor. I can't help putting myself in his place, in the forest, the night full of wolves.

I'll have to ask Grandma what it was a herd of exactly.

I tell myself first of all that his situation must have been much worse than ours. At least there are walls around me and Poulette. Maybe I could even barricade us by lifting and wedging the door across the threshold. And—what luxury!—in this hovel there's a chimney so I can make a fire.

Except no wood. Neither log nor twig. Our ancestor surely had everything he needed at hand. I couldn't plan ahead, I couldn't have anticipated this most recent setback.

It's too late to go to the woods to gather birch or oak.

On top of which, who's to say there are no more wolves? Huh!?

Wolves who, hunted down millennia after millennia, have become slyer and meaner than ever. Hiding in the depths of the forest, in remote tunnels, hidden burrows, only coming out on nights with a full moon.

Why would I abandon my Angélique all alone in our cottage in bumfuck nowhere only to wind up in the jaws of the descendants of those wolves who, unto the ages of ages, in the nearby woods, wanted to eat my poor little old ancestor?!

But who cares about the bundles of twigs, dear Fignole, if I may ask? There are more pressing matters at present than the lack of logs and dearth of twigs.

There is the unforgivable oversight of the flint.

If you're like me, you always have some flints in a drawer, a safe, a pocket, a koala, somewhere.

Just in case.

But I lapsed. I normally always have flint on me, but due to incredible distraction, a partially hereditary curse, my pockets are empty.

Ergo, even if I had a log, or birch, or twigs, I would have nothing to light my fire.

All that striving to act on our muddernizing ambitions, just to relapse to the age of caves, and maybe even further back, to the preflint era.

Best I can do is note on the tablets in my head to add flint to the czechlist of my standard equipment.

Angélique, my immured Poulette, I am seized with despair.

Do you not see that we strive, that we struggle in vain . . . We haul and we hoist, and then we slip, lapse, and regress all the way past the Styx, into prehistory, with neither fire nor pyre.

Tell me, O! tell me why . . .

Why is it that the more we try to muddernize, to yuppify, the more we crappify and wind up calcified up shit creek?

Shit creek! my mummy Poulette, shit creek! It's as though it is without a why . . .

So much so, my cute little mute, that blowing our brains out . . .

Except that'd be cowardly, huh!

We won't take the queasy way out.

Even if it's night, even if this scatastrophic setback catapults us back to the dawn of time.

We won't take the queasy way out.

But then what the hell do we do?

11.

Like a Ballerina

WHAT THE HELL DO WE do?

Hey, Poulette, how bout I tell some stories?

I could roll out the tablets I store in my head. To keep us from sinking into the pre-Paleolithic era, I could tell the stories of our glory days. Maybe that'd chase away the wolves and the terror of the dreaded doo-doo.

Do you remember, Angélique, our wars of times past?

It started with tournaments just like in the court of King Henry II.

Of course we didn't have horses, and the cows (which we had in abundance) didn't appreciate us mistaking their vocation. But we had bikes.

We didn't have any armor, let alone chain mail, but we had tubs of detergent and plenty of chicken wire.

Most importantly, we had helmets. Real ones.

Cause in the attic, before the attempt at muddernization, there were all sorts of relics from ancestral wars. In the steamer trunks there are scraps of period outfits. Combat uniforms in leopard and sky-blue camo. Even some incredible bright red pants. And fourragères, dog tags, medals, shoulder boards, beautiful bayonets (which our grandpa confiscated as soon as he saw them on our training ground).

We add to the patriotic debris—we embellish it!—with embroidered tablecloths that we use as capes, and ribbons to flap in the wind.

We deck ourselves out. And most importantly, we helmet it up. Before each battle, we draw straws for who gets the M51 and who gets the Adrian.

We don't go very far back in time, and also our family tree doesn't go up very high, so there are no helms or basinets in our trunk of heroic wonders. The right to gut and skin ourselves alive along the path to glory, the privilege of getting our brains blown out on the battlefield, these are brand-new conquests for us. Because our ancestors were all hicks till basically yesterday.

But that doesn't stop us from having our tournaments. In a surge of splendor, we even invited all the little neighborhood bumpkins to come and break a lance in our courtyard.

It'd be chichi and chivalrous, we'd hoped.

But the tournament degenerated into a brawl,

which degenerated into casus belli, which Angélique and I welcomed with delight.

It was a change from our civil wars.

Cause we like to wage war, she and I, but since she never wants to be the English or even the Krauts, and since it makes me too sad to always sacrifice myself and play the part of the hereditary enemy or the genocidal brute, Angélique and I decided very early on to be patriots concurrently.

By a formal treaty inscribed in two identical copies on our respective tablets (hers entrusted to the koala, mine in my head) and ratified on her birthday, we stipulated that we'd lie in wait, spar, fortify, steal, besiege, entrench, devastate, decimate—in sum carry out all operations and maneuvers, offensive and defensive alike, as civilly as possible.

So Angélique and I waged extravagant revolts, venomous wars of independence, atrocious wars of religion.

The prospect of uniting our forces against myriad enemies, unjust and brutal, led us to ratify an armistice on the spot, in two identical copies tacitly inscribed on tablets as soon as our rural tournament devolved.

Why did the tournament devolve?

Cause of one depraved kid, more depraved than we could've imagined when we launched urbi et orbi our invitation to a joust and an orderly massacre.

On foot, on baby goat, or on bike, all the village's

troops showed up in our courtyard while Grandma and Grandpa were taking their nap. The hamlets had heard we were throwing a joust for the ages. The cream of the crop of bumpkin nobility, every vassal and their uncle had rushed to our farm at the appointed hour.

All that was missing were the kids from the Castle, the ci-devant Crusaders. They come from an old family. They come from so far back that the marquis fell right into peenury's shit creek, and his son the baron even worse, into the manure pit that serves as the moat of the Castle, one day when he was dead drunk and tipped over like the itsy-tipsy spider.

But even without the barons, the baronets, or the spiders it was a beautiful spectacle. An onslaught of bicycles, rakes, and pitchfork handles.

Quite the mob.

Cause we're all bored stiff in the countryside, outside of the regular episodes of terror and muddernization.

Poulette and I had gathered farm benches as bleachers for guests who preferred to act like Ladies, because they wanted to or because the idea of rushing and pedaling at breakneck speed from one end of the courtyard, pitchfork or pickax handle wedged tightly under their armpit, straight for adversaries identically armed and identically pedaling, threw them into a panic.

Now, this one kid with a yellowish complexion didn't want to play a Lady but was clearly nearly shitting his pants at the thought of pedaling, so he got it in his head to act like a blue blood and insult a real Lady, a most dignified and beautiful Lady at that. And why? Because she was black, 100 percent black, with no pedigree since she came from the foster system and had washed up in the home of the poor old woman who lives by the river. And he (the yellow one) objected to her color and would not fight in the presence of such an ignoble creature.

The maliciousness, I have to admit, took me aback. I blushed.

The Lady froze, her eyes immense and gazing off into the distance. Her mute mouth contorted.

Angélique, who, for her part, was standing on the edge of the arena, at the foot of the bleachers, her main chick, the black hen, under her arm, foot tightly wedged into the raised pedal, spear in midair, chinstrap of her M51 buckled, ready to charge into the jousting field against the first scruffy hicks who showed their faces, Angélique was bewildered. I saw her stagger on her seat and, stunned, prop herself up on her pitchfork.

And I, in the face of such maliciousness, burning with shame that in my presence someone would dare insult the first Lady to grace our bleachers, no doubt the first black Lady to ever show up at a bicycle joust held on these grounds, I rushed to defend her honor, which had been insulted by that jaundiced jabroni.

Mounting my bike, tightly gripping the handlebars, I hoisted myself out of the saddle, dancing on the pedals like a ballerina.

I know, I know . . . dancing, ballerinas . . . unfortunate imagery . . .

But that's what it's called, and I may do the pedal dance but I'm no pansy pedo. Oh no, not I. In fact it was a masculine drive that spurred my pedaling.

And Angélique assures me that when I dance on the pedals I don't wiggle my ass even in the slightest.

My honor is intact.

So, dancing on my pedals, the top of my Adrian helmet all beribboned with madder red and sky blue, as I accelerate, I lower the pitchfork handle brooding under my left wing and swoop down on the glanderous yellow creep.

My spear pricked him in the sternum and sent him hillbilly ass over flea-ridden head onto the lawn.

Upon seeing which the neighbors, cousins, and vassals of the yellow jerk thought it wise to thrust their feet on the pedals and try their hand at charging into the melee.

Angélique, immediately grasping the strategic angle, swung her black hen very high in the air, and as it came down, flapping its stumpy wings, she snapped her beak and pedaled her talons onto the swarm of flea-ridden foulmouths, derailing half of them.

They piled up ungracefully in a jumble of grease-stained banners and ribbons.

An about-face, accomplished by a sharp braking and foot-dragging action, brought me back to the field, facing the tide of vassals following at my heels. Then, pitchfork handle held parallel to my handlebars, I rushed straight into the crowd, repeating to myself to boost my courage, Charge! Charge! On offense, always! And speed! And power!

Which has some truth to it, cause I carved a large breach in the enemy front, while Poulette, coming from the opposite direction, followed by one of our relatives and neighbors, a valiant rug rat astride her young racing goat, repressed the flanks of the vassal troop against the barn wall, where thighs and cheeks and elbows scratched and bled.

At last, Angélique, the rug rat, and I, dismounting, rushed to reach the enemy, swinging our sticks down onto ribs and asses and feet. And soon we laid a heap of broken spears and countless hillbillies, groaning and bloody, at the feet of our Lady, who was petrified with admiration.

To top it off, Angélique reweaponized her chick, who pecked at all the ears, armpits, and eyes she could find.

Our Lady was dumbstruck. We'd laid waste to the entire army of her tormentors.

She was the only Lady remaining. All the others, boys and girls, had vanished at the first drop of blood.

We plop onto the grass, Poulette, the rug rat, the kid, the chicken, the Lady, and I. We prepare ourselves a delicious snack, foraged from Grandma's pantry. We spread fromage blanc on big slices of bread and shave bits of bitter chocolate on top. It's dee-vine.

Our Lady is named Catherine. She's skinny, from her arms to her legs.

The jaundiced jamoke, who's so big and fat that the grime encrusted in parallel lines in the folds of his neck forms a musical staff with his acne marking quavers and rests, the jamoke's been causing problems for our Lady since Child Services placed her in the old woman's home by the river. He doesn't want anyone to play with her. He taunts her, saying face like coal, come lick this pole.

Which cracks up his vassals.

So we adopted our unlucky Lady, unanimously, without even anticipating the exploits and pas d'armes she'd inspire in us.

Remember, Poulette?

That time we went to free her from captivity in the dump where the neighboring farmer ties up his dog under the nasty sheet metal roof?

Remember when we had her play, in succession, Anne of Austria, Constance Bonacieux, and Milady de Winter?

She agreed to give us her diamond pendants.

She didn't object to ironing d'Artagnan's shirts (that's me, d'Artagnan).

But when we decided to take her out on the pond in a boat one foggy day, and we ripped her dress to reveal the scar on her shoulder, she screamed.

Shiny tears streamed down her poor thin cheeks.

It was a heck of a scene.

Do you remember, Athos? (That's you! Poulette!)

We strained to remember that she was a traitress despite her tears.

Poulette, you had been her lover ages ago! You had just come out of a monastery, situated for the convenience of the narrative in our barn . . . do you remember? Athos! You were moved, somber and mute. Hunched over your rapier, you kept your eyes on the wake as I rowed our boat away from the bank, but not so farts that we would risk washing up on the spillway amidst the fog and tears.

In her lacerated dress, Milady wailed lacerating cries.

She held around her skinny little shoulders the scraps that revealed nothing but protruding bones, not a single dishonorable scar.

We tried to remain steadfast.

We had planned on dumping her into the lake, our Milady, so we could then heroically save her from the mud and the sludge. We would have administered first aid to her on the bank.

But we were suffering.

I saw your resolve, Athos—do you remember?—weaken in the face of Milady's tears. And I, I clenched my fists around the oars and gritted my teeth against my sobs, no longer knowing whether it was my Lady or Milady I was torturing.

A real fucking dilemma.

Frozen stiff in her rag, shivering, she finally cried, Mercy! Mercy! And with that word, I don't know why, we burst into tears, Angélique, d'Artagnan, Athos, and I.

We fell into each other's arms. We embraced. We bathed in reciprocal tears.

I offered her my shirt (which she'd freshly ironed) on the spot, humid with the fog and the sweat of rowing. I made a U-turn and headed for the bank, so fast that when we hit it the pontoon went flying and we almost shipwrecked.

Around the kitchen table, under the lamp, because the fog outside overshadows the day, we snack.

Lady Catherine is wearing a dress that Angélique gave her as formal reparation for the affront to her own. She takes a long time eating. She chews slowly. So slowly she falls asleep as she's eating. And continues to chew as she sleeps.

She cried so much because the dress was her only

one, and now Grandma, sitting at the sewing machine, is solidly patching it up for her.

Once the dress is mended, we company Catherine back to the old woman's home by the river. Can't let her be ambushed in her brand-new dress by the jaundiced dingus.

On the way, she tells us of her misfortunes.

She has no memory of a family. Before, she was in a prison with pedagogues and other kids who tormented her. She begged to be released. That's why they sent her to the countryside, to the middle of nowhere, to live with the old woman.

She milks the cow, morning and night. She wheelbarrows the manure. She takes the poor beast to pasture. She polishes the saucepans and eats the scraps. She sleeps in the poor woman's attic, and at night, when the bats take flight, she hides her head under the sheet. But it's better than prison.

How did they torment her in prison? we ask her.

Her mouth contorts. Her eyes widen.

12.

We Don't Give a Clam

WE'LL NEVER KNOW HOW . . . cause her mouth contorts and she goes quiet. Her eyes widen and stare off into the hedges at the side of the road.

We don't push it.

We wage war.

Once and for all, we must defeat the yellow felon.

Galloping behind bovines, tipping over the calves asleep in the barn, racing our bikes through farmyards to scramble the poultry, we have no more time for that. No more desire. We ditch the cows. The rodeos, the westerns, that's all over now.

We devote ourselves to our study of the military arts. Every morning we scrutinize the stray volumes of an old encyclopedia. Poulette, the koala, and I ponder a worm-eaten illustrated volume on the Boer War. We even pore over an old catechism, in case it contains biblical battle plans. Sieges, wars of liberation, pitched battles, colonial campaigns, cavalry charges, or armored divisions maneuvers. All we find we glean and boil down to maxims.

The rest of the time, we see to armament and training. We have hazel sticks aplenty drying in the barn. We gather all the puffball mushrooms we can find, the really ripe ones, and store them in paper bags in the cellar. We steal rakes from all the surrounding farms. We shelter our stash of firecrackers leftover from the fourteenth of July.

And then we fine-tune and test our secret weapon, our ultimate weapon: the dung bomb.

The dung bomb, perfected by me, is a projectile with a wide cone of fire, a suffocating poison gas, and a biological weapon all in one. Clearly by no means a conventional weapon, and the international treaties are silent about it.

Developed, as its name indicates, from semidry cow dung, it's a formidable weapon, but quite delicate to handle.

We go around noon to collect them on the road where they've had time to dry after the cows have deposited them on the way between the pasture and the barn and back. They reek all the more when the bovines have been fed silage. We know the right places, the best barns. Dry and rigid on top—the air-dried side—and wet on the underside.

The tricky part is collecting them without soiling yourself; the key is to stockpile them on crates without letting them dry out too much, and without alarming Grandma, who sees us mucking about with these shit-cakes morning and night and wonders what on earth we could be doing with so much manure.

The dung bomb can be deployed at short and long range, preferably with a badminton racket. Controlling the trajectory is an art unto itself, but Poulette and I never falter, never flag during training. We do it as discreetly as possible, cause we don't want to perturb our grandparents. We've pebble-dashed the back wall of the barn in a rustic, rammed-earth style. Poulette assures me that's how they do it in some traditional cultures. Seen from afar and from up close, it's unique, conspicuous. But weirdly, in a thin layer, it stinks less than you might think.

There have been skirmishes.

We've come under fire. The kin and allies of the nasty yellow felon throw stones at us. But they're too far away. They don't even come close. And, since the tournament that devolved, Poulette and I are always on high alert. We don't leave the house without our helmets and armor.

Taking fire, facing off against scattered projectiles, usually we dismount and Poulette, the black hen, and I do a jig, all three of us arm in arm, singing at the top of our lungs and as flat as possible.

It disconcerts the enemy!

It screws with their shots!

We sing the national rural anthem, which we composed one rainy afternoon to the tune of "Dans un amphithéatre." It goes like this:

All their liddle stones, liddle stones, liddle stones, ah we don't give a duck, give a duck, give a duck, honk honk! Aaah bout the liddle hands, of those big hairy schmucks, hairy schmucks, hairy schmucks, honk honk!

Aaand their lousy salvo, zee salvo, honk honk, we just don't give a toot, give a toot, give a toot.

Theeey whip out their big guns, their big guns, we laugh our glasses off, glasses off, glasses off.

Aaand as for the Krauts, we don't give a clam, give a clam, not even a cat's ass, a rat's ass, a bat's ass, honk honk!

But it doesn't even rhyme! you say . . .

Well guess what! As for the rhyme, we don't give, we don't give a what? We don't give a ham or a clam.

It's not poetic enough either?

You know what? We don't care about the poetry, we don't give a cuck or a truck of you know what.

Honk honk!

After the last couplet, we get back in the saddle. Angélique crams her black hen into the basket. We tighten our chinstraps and prepare to charge straight down the hill, freewheeling and screaming Banzai! and then Montjoie my asshole! and then Goddammit!

It never fails to make an impression: the troops perk up before we reach the bottom of the hill and turn onto the first hollow road to cut across the fields and reach our barns and shelters.

Finally, the rumor spread that the yellow felon was planning to come looking for trouble and kick our asses on our own land. Basically, that he was preparing an attack on our farm. Lady Catherine came running and panting from the other end of the village to warn us.

We'd noticed the yellow eunuchoid thug expanding his recon into our vicinity. We saw him coming from afar in his big rubber clogs.

(Cause no one wears wooden shoes anymore, not even in our village . . . Except our grandpa . . . And even he only wears them at night, when it's dark, to do his rounds and close the shutters.

Dusk must seize him with nostalgia for times past.

He wears the clogs sparingly and keeps them hidden away, sheltered from our muddernizing curiosities. Cause there's no one left to fix them up for him, a little slash with the drawknife here, rasp a little bump in the sole there, or even just make him a new pair. Clogmaker isn't a profession you see anymore.)

Anyway, the yellow felon, we saw him coming from

a distance with his big rubber clogs the color of fresh manure, determined to stomp on our faces with them.

This might be the only time in our lives when Angélique and I ever wished our lineage dated back to the Crusades. It would have been so easy to withstand the siege of the Castle . . . The Castle was built for that exact purpose, even if amidst the general decadence, especially the decadence of those high and mighty aristocrats, windows were foolishly cut in the walls, vistas were opened, stoops installed, and the dungeons turned into rococo extravaganzas.

We surveyed the perimeter. With the cooperation of the koala and Lady Catherine, we outlined plans, surveyed the terrain. We pondered.

Fortifying our barn was too hairy a proposition. Given our time constraints, Vauban himself would have given up.

What we needed wasn't a rococo extravaganza. What we needed was the opposite of muddernization.

We had to medievalize.

On two of its sides—escarpment, massive metal gate—our farm is unassailable, thanks to our adversary's lack of technical and tactical abilities.

But to the north and to the east, the sad truth is that an invasion, even a simple incursion, could slice easy as through butter (freshly churned, compact but soft). There's a tiny stream you can cross like the

Rubicon. There's a little ancient wall, collapsed, ridiculous. There's a bit of barbed wire enclosure to keep in the cows. In other words, zilch.

Northern Front, Eastern Front: why do invasions always come from one of those two sides?

Angélique, hen, and I are not going to dig trenches. Too many bad memories from the trenches. We lost too many good men who wound up etched on the face of patriotic monuments.

Poulette and I, the two of us together are barely worth our weight in cannon fodder. We'd need cousins and nephews, godchildren and kin . . . We'd need numerous and extended families, luxurious genealogical canopies, entire forests . . .

Which aren't so common anymore . . . Having gone out of fashion actually since the aforementioned trench times, which trenchantly cut the generation to the quick, lineage slashed, spawn all gone.

We no longer have the demographics for those kinds of wars. It's a real shame.

We won't be foolish enough to fall for another Maginot. We know all too well how easily outflanked a static defensive line can be.

Defense! That's the problem! We're not accustomed to being on the defensive.

We'd have to use the element of surprise, speed, mobility. That's what you suggested, Poulette. Pin the adversary on our most naturally advantageous side. Concentrate all our strength on the other front, the main front, where we'd lure the majority of the enemy divisions by pretending to leave it unguarded. Swiftly throw all our forces into battle there, capitalizing on the superiority of our field artillery. Once this first army corps is sent running, we'll turn around in a dazzling maneuver, concentrating all our forces on a strategic post to wage the ultimate fight.

I reminded you, Poulette, of the virtues of strategic depth. Which was provided to us by our most inhospitable wasteland, the one bordering the Eastern Front. A former orchard, never cleared, sprouting basal shoots galore in an incredible vegetal delirium. A dense jungle, a pocket-sized Indochina, a thick thicket of brambles and interlaced shrubs.

Let the enemy venture into this dense desert, and we'll take him from behind in a classic turnabout moment.

We'll hound him! We'll crush him! We'll demoralize him!

We'll throw Bonaparte in bed with Giáp and Kutuzov.

Perched high in the eaves of the hangar, I was keeping watch, observing the surroundings through my binoculars via a hole in the roof, when I heard clusters of whippersnappers start to detonate (those little firecrappers that go bang-snap undersole when trodden on), which we'd scattered over the country road to sound the alarm at the first incursion.

Since we didn't have a bugle, I sounded the call to arms on our loudest cooking pot. I noted the presence of an enemy column on the border of the wasteland, to the east, and of another hustling amidst the wild mint on the right bank of the Rubicon. Then I tumbled down from my observation post quick as I could.

Poulette had already reached our frontline behind the little wall that anchors our Northern Front, double-fisting badminton rackets loaded up with puffball mushrooms ready to pulverize. She launches them at once with ballistic delectation and precision while I draw CRÉCY! my bow and begin to shoot POITIERS! a full quiver of hazel sticks, nice and sharp. I rain down AGINCOURT! strikes at sustained rate into the grass bordering the brook to dislodge the rival troops hiding there.

The first wave of assailants rears its head by the stream.

This is the critical moment, the moment to unleash our stash of dung bombs. Let's paint these Krauts from top to bottom.

We trebuchet our six badminton rackets, one after the other. Lady Catherine and our cousin (the kid racer) are in charge of the crates stored in the barn. They reload the dung and serve up the rackets ready for use through the basement window.

Rolling artillery barrage!

Rapid rate of fire!

Our dung bombs pebble-dash and pin the enemy ranks.

Coming in at a nosedive, the dung splatters their boots, seeps down their shirt collars.

When a lobbed dung bomb hits a foot soldier right in the kisser, the impact is instantaneous. He closes his eyes, closes his mouth, stops breathing. His hands drop the pitchfork, the pickax, the pebble. He starts frantically wiping himself, and the more he wipes, the more he spreads the crap. And the more crap he spreads, the less he dares open his eyes and the more he crashes into the rest of his regiment.

Our barrage of dung bombs has sown complete chaos on the Northern Front.

It's time to make our move.

We grab the loaded cartridge belts and shoulder the knapsacks packed with the biggest July fourteenth firecrackers we could find.

We padlock the barn so the enemy can't raid our dung bomb stash.

We whistle for the kid. Cousin mounts it bareback.

We straddle our bikes.

We move.

We hurtle down the scree and rush at full speed towards the Rubicon. We ride through the disbanded blinded ranks of Krauts on the Northern Front and dole out pitchfork strikes to all the backs that dare show themselves. But we have no time to waste on a proper corrida, nor to fine-tune the defeat of the Teutonic brutes.

Let them wander up to their eyes in shit creek until the cows come home, and that'll do! Yes, that'll do!

We heil-tail it back up the left bank of the Rubicon. It's the turnabout moment I envisioned, and now we're bunkered behind the lines of the Eastern Front's wilderness, into which did tread, as predicted, the second army corps of the vile yellow felon.

We pull our stash of jam jars from a cache in the bramble bush.

Secret weapons. Strategically positioned ahead of time.

Cause we'd climbed up to the attic the day before yesterday to collect all the spiders we could find, giant hairy ones and little mean ones too. Now we shake up the jars where the famished beasties are moping around. We agitate them and we dump them into the basket of badminton shuttlecocks that we immediately parabola into the jungle. We alternate with the firecrackers, which Catherine and Poulette light and lob like grenades. We set them off far and wide. We let the gunpowder do the talking and we rain black widows through the canopy.

We hear the first screams. We glimpse panicked galloping through the high grass. And then the onslaught heard round the world: the WHACK! THUD! of the rakes we'd scattered throughout the wilderness, turning it into a real minefield. Our galloping Huns tread on the rakes and get a magisterial pole to the schnoz.

Some are knocked stiff.

Some cry for help, for aid, whining and calling for their mommies.

Some gallop even faster.

They stamp, terrified, through the grass and crash into a wasp's nest. Stung all over, they throw themselves against the pear trees grown wild, the bushy blackthorns with their vicious little spikes. They dive into curtains of brambles. They crawl frantically through the hedges to regain their native pasture and escape the vegetal, insect-ridden, and explosive hell into which they've been lured by the yellow felon.

Who was lying, schnoz bleeding, passed out at the foot of a pear tree. How you like them apples?

We didn't kill him.

It was when we tried to medic him that things almost turned doggone hairy for him. He saw himself all lathered with antiseptic and iodine and thought he was dead. He reswooned on the spot, among the bruised apples and the bitter wild pears, and even worse: into complete dogalepsy.

I'll admit it, we were humming to ourselves as we coddled and palpated him with bandaging gauze. Mean yellow fellow, I'll pummel you and fuck you up, up to your eyes, to your eyes. Mean yellow fellow, to your eyes, to your eyes, roll over! I'll trick your ass and chuck your berries . . .

He was grinding his gums. A string of pink drool trickled out of him, which became lattices and bubbles, so much was he foaming.

We didn't kill him. We didn't rob him. We didn't torture him either. As the chick is my witness! And the kid too!

We didn't even chuck him in Gitmo.

We could've held him prisoner. We have the perfect cellar for it, in our vast annexes. A cellar that's totally empty, wet, and full of spiders. A real medieval dungeon that'd turn our ci-devant lords and even our historical allies the Americunts green with envy.

We made him sign an unconditional surrender, a humiliating capitulation. We made him swear to disband his battalions. We made him deliver a formal apology to Lady Catherine, grovel on his knees, lick her feet.

Our Lady wasn't quite keen on this ceremony. We

had to insist. The nasty yellow felon was resigned. He spinelessly and conscientiously licked the toes we presented to him.

He promised that from now on he'd dedicate himself exclusively to farming and would never again wield his pitchfork at anything other than hay, straw, or manure.

We sent him back on the road to his hamlet. Cause he'd lost his way, the sad hepatic antiseptized and iodized idiot. He kept heading down the alley to the Castle, as if intent on going for a bath in the manure pit of the former Crusaders.

We didn't take him prisoner cause we hate captivity more than anything.

If to live vanquished and without glory is to die each day, to live as a captive is to teem like a dead rat in the rank moat of time.

13.

Blinkskrieg

HENS WHY I SO DREAD returning to the city at summer's end, at the start of the school year.

In the city, we're prey to the guardians of discipline. They chuck us into centers to air us out. They conserve us in conservatories. They inculcate and incarcerate us, so much that it feels like a Calvary. Since the day they tossed me into my school prison I've been trying to escape.

But the walls are too high, too smooth to scale. I'd accelerate to attempt a vertical gallop like Bruce Lee or Jet Li, Zhang Ziyi or Neo in their dojos, and I'd fall back down like a sack of taters.

And the door (I didn't think of the door until later, I'll admit), once I thought of it, I quickly saw it was guarded all day by a witch on a broomstick, a monstrous woman who was not at all easygoing, with eyes in the back of her head and also in her earholes and even between her kneecaps . . . cause when I tried to discreetly commando-crawl in front of her post to the street exit, I wound up in the principal's office.

I thought of a grappling hook. I dreamed of a sleeping potion. Then I finally settled on a desperate plan, cause nothing was working and you, Angélique, you didn't mind school . . . so try as I might to badger you about escaping, you don't give, don't give an I don't know what.

One morning, I went to school with my leg all rigid, claiming a nasty fall and swollen knee. But my leg was only stiff cause I'd hidden a crowbar in my pants, one I'd stolen from the family toolbox. The crowbar was my get-out-of-jail-free card, I was already imagining myself on the outside. Farewell putrid pedagogues, stagnant boredom, sadistic guard dogs!

I was going to escape, and in the same way as all the greats: through the sewers! Cause there's no other path to take to get out of prison, the barracks, the penal colony, the barricade, even Château d'If.

That's when the teachers stopped me, just as I'd dislodged the giant cast-iron slab at the far end of the playground and was tuckering myself out trying to lift it without ampootating my toes.

The bastards! Those daughters and sons of snitches! They confiscated my crowbar!

I cried bitter tears over it all day long. I begged for

my crowbar. I promised to never again try to slide down that manhole. (There's another one, a littler one, near the toilets. I made a mental note . . .)

Ever since that day, Poulette, you've been asking me every night, and I never know if it's out of concern or sarcasm, you ask me, Fignole, my darling, did you cry at school today?

I always answer no, I didn't have time.

And you know why, Poulette?

Cause I learned, after they cruelly ampootated my crowbar, I learned to escape in my head.

I can even escape in the middle of the day now. I settle behind my desk and gallop silently in my head.

My teachers all end up noticing sooner or later that I'm escaping in my head. They ask me, Are you in dreamland?!

Yes, I'm dreaming. Of war and defective conjugations, of destructions, devastations, capitulations. I dig holes in grammar and I concoct escapes, scalings, resurrections, and descents into the sewers.

That's what I do in town.

In town everything is already so muddern . . . All those telethings, all those electrons, those photons shut up in boxes, tied up with cables, zooming visions and voices. Waves and particles that vroom at full speed through circuits so nanoscopic that when they get fucked it's not even worth trying to repair them.

Doomed to the dumpster.

My heart bleeds for all those poor wasted machines and sorry thingies.

And no concrete! At best, on rare occasions, the pleasures of demolition. Like the time, one Saturday afternoon, before our mother came home, when our father got it in his head to expand the living room by knocking down the dividing wall that separated it from the dining room.

I say dividing wall, but it was made of good solid concrete, and our father had to take the sledgehammer to it. Happily. You could tell he'd been waiting for months to go balls to the wall.

You're sure it's not a load-bearing wall? Angélique asked him, highly suspicious of the utility of this demolition.

We'll find out, he said.

Angélique and I gathered the rubble like ball kids at Roland-Garros. Between two sledgehammer strikes, being extremely careful to avoid a mishap, we ran to collect the debris in a pink basin that we took in heaps to the bathtub (which groaned, soon filled up, and then overflowed . . .).

Such an undertaking creates a lot of noise and debris.

An ocean of rubble.

How to get rid of it without filling all the building

trash cans? We loaded our pockets with rubble, which we discreetly dropped into park sandboxes, into flowerbeds, into construction site dumpsters, under market stalls.

As for the noise . . .

The neighbors, shut up in their living rooms, their bedrooms, didn't dare call the cops or the firefighters or even an ambulance, in case the savage mason, the active chuter on the third floor, decided to take his sledgehammer to their adjoining walls, their ceiling, or their front door. Trembling, breathing a sigh or a little cry at each thrash that sent their chandeliers wobbling, warped the doors in their frames, and made the closet doors slam, they waited. They hoped for sudden fatigue, for the munchies, for our mother's return, a lovely lady, and so discreet . . .

You should see our neighbors' terror, ever since that deranged Saturday, whenever they run into our father in the elevator and he turns, pleasantly, to shake their hand.

Very courteous brutes, washed, waxed, and buffed savages, gorillas in their Sunday best, that's how they see us in our building. And even beyond, in the entire neighborhood, thanks to our exploits at school, Poulette and me.

Cause the only thing that never changes, in town or on the farm, is the state of war. You think war is the exception. Well you're wrong, dead wrong. Kidding yourselves. Delusional. As History teaches us, peace is the rarity.

But with all the concretes we'd poured, all the blows we'd doled out in our rural wars, Angélique and I had gained speed, muscle, lethal precision.

All the more cause in the countryside the Krauts are no pansies. Not like in the big city. All the kids in school have spent their summers at computer camp, on linguistic trips to some sissy country, on cultural exchange with the Pygmies. They've sampled sliced-up schnauzer in Sydney, savored soy-sauced locust livers in Shanghai, tasted tortoise tortillas in Timbuktu, partaken in python en papillote with the Papuans, bitten into brilliant barbecued brochettes in Bali, lapped up warthog brain in Ouarzazate alongside Lapland migrants.

Result: we faced off against a bunch of petty-bourgeois bastards. My little sis won a dozen arm wrestling tournaments in a row without breaking a sweat. We won so much pocket money our first day back at school with the bets I took banking on Poulette's biceps . . .

We wiped the floor with those lowlifes. That's why they didn't like us. Sneaky and cowardly. Real bourgeois tramps.

The problem is they became wary. Hereditarily fearing beatings, they fled. But vicious as they were, they couldn't enjoy life without picking on someone. As though it were necessary for their equilibrium and if they didn't they might turn anemic. So the lowlifes picked on the weaker than us and the smaller than them.

That's how they ended up joining forces against a little sissy who didn't have the advantage of a rural background or an exotic, expensive education.

Have to mention that the little sissy lived with his widow mother in a caretaker's lodge, and he wasn't even Portuguese.

He'd atrophied all summer in a stairwell, longing for fresh air and bringing the mail up to the various floors. He'd brooded over braised lettuce, boiled turnips, cauliflower in a meager gratin, alley cat crackling.

And so, in a corner of the playground, our lappers of simian scallion cornered the little sissy who wasn't even Portuguese to introduce him to superior gastronomy. Oh he was gonna eat, the poor little thing raised on braised lettuce. First a tartare of big fat worms imported directly from the yard flowerbeds, followed by a chiffonade of spiders. Unless he preferred a knuckle sandwich instead.

Poulette caught wind of the ruse and sounded the alarm. I hustled over from the other end of the playground.

Nach Berlin!!! Full speed ahead!!!

When they saw us, the swine stuffed their

confections into the little sissy's pockets and shoved him aside, then seemed to hesitate. They struck decorative poses, the swine. And then assumed the supremely bored expressions of people who've been bothered at teatime by a general mobilization.

My little sis gave them an ultimatum. Release the little sissy or else, no mercy.

The swine were wary. They hesitated.

They feared reprisals once the hostage was handed over. They wanted assurances.

So my little sis hurled insults at them. She must run drills in her head, or else she has a special tablet to write down the intriguing indignities that fall into her lap or come to her mind.

With the bourgeois, it's not hard.

The bourgeois think vocabulary belongs to them. Even when they don't understand fuck all. Especially when they don't understand fuck all. One ironic word and they think they're being called moronic. One recondite phrase and suddenly, it's some dumb slander.

The swine had no clue about Poulette's strategic doctrine.

They planted their hands in front of their balls, girding them like a Vaginot line, thinking that was where we'd invade. They were all lined up like toy soldiers, two mitts on their zippers and knees squeezed tight.

They were cupping their balls, and turning a blind

eye to everything else, but it was preslicely there, in their eyes, that my little sis stuck her fingers.

Bombs away! I screamed.

Right in the eyes, first Poulette got 'em with several powerful spitgobs to cloud their vision.

We made it rain into their eyes. Once they were good and cloudy, we unloaded.

Poulette, who developed this strategy, calls it Blinkskrieg.

They think a blow to the balls is the most painful thing. When they take a hit to the eyes, they revise their position: maybe that's what hurts the most.

It's a fascinating seesaw, as is the effect it has on the human mind, specially the bourgeois mind. We were presented with a rare opportunity to run a methodical experiment.

I set my sights on a pair, the worst and the whiniest of the bunch, to figure out what they'd end up holding the tightest, their balls or their eyeballs, by the end of a leisurely and iterated alternating strike. They had a pair of each, the pair of them. They'd have to choose.

They hesitated, those bourgeois ball jugglers.

So I persisted, distributing my blows equitably but randomly between the one and the other, their balls and their eyeballs, up, down, left, right.

They hesitated. But it's cause they had only two mitts, the swine... always one step behind, ever exposed, unable to decide on one organ or the other. Which only causes them more suffering, those Buridan's asses, said Angélique, who is clever albeit a bit cryptic sometimes.

Who's Buridan? I asked her.

The husband of Occam's sister, she responded. Basically, an auntie . . .

In the end, we pulled the little sissy out from under the heap of blinded countertenors. We emptied his pockets of all the sticky stuff the swine had shoved inside. We wiped his nose, cause after so much crying there was snot streaming from it and such misery was revolting.

There were complaints from parents whose disinfectant, bandaging gauze, and Band-Aid costs skyrocketed. We were savages wrecking their progeny.

Our disinfectant of choice is iodized alcohol. It hurts but it's very efficient, much more so than those other pansy remedies. A little lidocaine here, some gentle antibiotics there, and in no time you've got gaseous gangrene.

Angélique and I never tire of bitch-slapping the bourgeois. It's a sport more fun and more honorable than bitch-slapping sissies.

Besides, sissies aren't always what you think. (The bourgeois, on the other hand, are always what you think.)

Max, for example, the little sissy we saved, who

never left our side after that, Max was snot such a sissy after all. The proof: he fell madly in love with Angélique. It was revolting, at least as much as the mucus that drips from his nose three days out of five (the other two his sinuses are stuffed up and he begs us to give him a good wallop so his snot will deign to hurtle down his septum).

And on that note, you won't believe it, but our father was bequeefed an inheritance from a sissy, a real one.

14.

The Pansy's Bequest

A CERTIFIED PANSY. SUCH A namby and such a pamby that he got himself killed by another pedo, less of a pansy pedo than him, who didn't want to pansy around or do the pedal dance and crapped out halfway down the fatal slope.

Or else the pedo was even more of a cream puff than him, and that's why he offed him. Who knows?

In any event, when the notary showed our father the will, it was indeed written that he, Philippe Oberkampf, was the universal and particular legatee of the fallen fruitcake, Virgile Froissart.

"Virgile, you know him?" Poulette asked.

"Virgile? No . . ." said our father. "In the penal colony, we called him Fagarotti."

"And what was your nickname?"

"Harmony, why?"

"Why Harmony?"

I would never've believed it, said our father. I used to herd the cows with him. I would never've believed he was such a nancy boy, that bumpkin. That music lover.

Music mellows murders. The deceased, he used to cruise at the opera. And it was another music lover who ripped another hole in him. Seventy-eight stab wounds, to be exact.

I would never've believed it, said our father. We herded the cows together. We gathered potatoes. We were on shitter duty. We were in custody. We were crook comrades, Fagarootti and I. We pitched each other's tents. How could this happen?

Maybe it's cause watching over cows and lusting after divas are different ball games. Coring apples and encoring string quartets don't call upon the same reflexes. Making that leap from the barn to the opera must've really done in his noggin and discombobulated the gay matter in Fagartootti's head. More than leaping through an airplane door, see ya!, feetfirst into the void.

After the surprise, the shame, the embarrassment of inheriting from the deceased de cujus, our father decided to go examine his legacy, de visu and in situ.

In the middle of the night, we take off, him and us.

In the back seat, Angélique sleeps gripping her you know what. Between her thumb and index finger she's holding the best part of Mr. Koala. It's a little silk scrap, pink like a panting dog tongue, that Grandma sewed in the animal's right ear. It's very soft, so soft that Angélique can't fall asleep without caressing and kneading Mr. Koala's ear between her fingers. Which is also why she won't let anyone trim her nails: it coarsens the creature's ear and compromises its softness.

I don't sleep. I pretend to.

Our father listens to a lecture on his tape deck. It's about war and nuclear bombs, civil panics and triage of the wounded. Those who're fucked straightaway, those who're fucked only halfway but who'll cost a lot in care, and then those who can be perked up enough to allegro smorzando get shot up with some more holes, dismembered, wrung out, vaporized, and killed all over again.

This gives me an idea, which I fine-tune in my head, to build myself a shelter, a concrete sarcophagus fortified with lead, a bulletproof Boche blockhouse like the one I saw when our family went to the coast. One day, when I've saved enough, I'll buy one, a blockhouse . . . I just hope it won't be too late.

Except I don't know if they're for sale, or which notary to get one from.

I'll stock it full of provisions to refuge myself with Grandma before the bomb drops on us. With my grandma cause she'll let me tweak, tinker, and sleep late. Even if there're no more mornings after the bomb's blasted everything, and probably not much left to tinker with. We'll still be able to talk, she and I, deep into the great nuclear night as we often do now when the others are asleep and I slide into her bed.

We drive, we drive until we reach a snowy valley, a deserted village, an austere hovel.

It was the end of the world, or almost.

We did the last two hundred yards on foot cause the slope was so steep and icy.

So this was where our father used to vacation with the assassinated ass-bandit. Vacations that consisted of herding cows and yanking potatoes.

Our father, he'd never hoped for the joy of inheriting anything. He had nothing to his name. And now he was the owner of something sturdy and solid, and it delighted him. He must've yearned for it for so long. It was obvious when he strode through the small garden and pushed open the door.

We climb upstairs on a steep ladder, groping our way through the deep darkness.

No rococo extravaganza. This inheritance is massively lacking in windows.

Empty room. Bare floor.

Alcove in a crude wall. Worm-eaten beds that collapse if you glance in their direction.

Fireplace, andiron, verdigris pot hanging from a soot-black hook.

Cold as all hell.

But a sound roof! Floorboards free from rot!

In the mountains, warns our father, at the bottom of the valley, night falls all at once. The sun dips behind a crest, it makes the opposite crest glimmer for a brief moment. The waning sky pinks, and then it's night and the brutal cold jumps you and freezes your bones.

So we rush out to fetch bales of hay from a barn that Poulette spotted. Since there's no one to pay, we leave a fifty on a pitchfork.

We pull out sheets and covers from the only armoire in Fagornotti's hovel. The sheets are damp, the covers made from thick wool and saturated with camphor.

At least we won't be eaten by moths.

We'll sleep on the hay. And for added warmth, maybe we'll sleep in the hay.

We light up our abode with a hurricane lantern. Our father has to suck gas from the tank of our car to refill the lantern. Angélique worries that after all those suctions, on top of the probable initial shortage, we won't be able to leave ever again and we'll be doomed to finish our days on the hay, at the quasi-end of the world, in the opposite of a rococo extravaganza.

We bury ourselves in the hay, beanies on our heads, and socks, and mittens. All knitted by our grandma, who has great foresight.

We play cards, mittens on our hands. A game

Poulette invented after reading an old psychiatry manual and stored by Mr. Koala for emergency distractions.

From the family of psychoses, I ask for erotomania. Cause paranoia, Cotard's delusion, I don't know why, always ends up in my hand. General paralysis, with its complete suite of causes, is Poulette's specialty. She inherits it every other time, along with congenital syphilis. Our father likes to do three of a kinds with his symptoms: hypnagogia, catatonia, hypomania.

This is how we spend our nights, after the soup and the sardines straight from the tin.

There's an outhouse at the end of the little garden. But at night, since it would mean risking death to venture outside: chamber pots! There was a whole collection of them, made from chipped earthenware or slightly dented enameled sheet metal, under the wreckage of the bed.

We each have our own.

Luxury, says our father.

In the morning, we clean up only where necessary, where it's dirty. It's a waste to wash where it's clean. In any case we'd have to break the ice floe over the bucket to be able to dip in a washcloth. And it's a long way to get water from the river.

While our father takes stock of his property, strolls, draws up plans, imagines future refurbishments, Angélique and I construct a fort to bolster the defense of the grounds. With an adjoining igloo. It requires back-breaking backfilling work, but once it's done we control the narrow communal road down below.

Since there's no shortage of tools in the deceased's hovel, we make a catapult using a shovel. We stockpile snowballs.

Poulette and I brought an entire arsenal in our luggage. The M16 grenade launcher, the Winchester repeater rifle that can shoot gravel. The Colts, the Lugers.

Guns—that's our Christmas. Santa never fails to add to our arsenal. Also, while our father was filling the shopping cart with canned food at the nearest supermarket, Poulette snuck off to find rolls, strips, and ring caps for all our weapons. He didn't even bat an eye when we met him at the register with all that powder.

We camouflage ourselves in prone position under a nice white sheet. We survey the mountain passes. We scrutinize the peaks. We await the adversary's offensive, which will surely materialize sooner or later.

But nobody shows up. Nothing happens. Not a cow, not a hick. Nothing, nothing but white. Nothing but the blinding white. Not a single band of old pillagers. Just a smoking chimney, to the right, on the frozen slope leading to the river and the road.

We decide to patrol the village, cautiously. We scale snowdrifts. We skim moraine walls. We look out for snipers lying in ambush.

Not a cat in the streets, not a rat on the roofs. No one on the winding country roads in the distance, snowy, bordered by low walls of dark stone. We pull bobbins on all the doors but not a single latch blows up.

The stables are empty. Worse: they're clean! Cold! They don't even smell of manure, that good warm muck.

Morning, we get excited at the sight of tracks along the river. In the snowy white, those little holes of shadow that trace a path, a trail . . . Angélique goes out to scout and comes back to report that all she's found are fox tracks and a red herring.

Not even a wolf.

We scrutinized all the peaks, all the cavernous shadows stretched across the steep rocky slopes.

We perfected our bastions, our redoubts, we reinforced buffer zones, erected curtain walls. Our igloo's no longer a fort, it's a citadel. Redoubted, bastioned like you wouldn't believe.

We don't even lie down anymore under our shrouds. What's the point of camouflaging yourself when there's no one spying on you?

We skirmish only skimpily. We sink into white torpor. We yawn in the middle of the day. Our eyes turn red and watery despite our ski goggles. Not a soul stirs. Not a dusting of snow, not a single flake escapes the goffering of ice. Only stalactites flaring from the gutters.

We mill about. We wait. We vacate. We wander. We idle.

We procrastinate: should we deploy?

Waiting is worse than fighting. Boredom leads to delirium. We hallucinate. We think we see Moors, Vikings, Normans, Hannibal and his elephants, Genghis Khan and the fellagha over yonder, charging at us from between two peaks.

We open fire, screaming at the intense prosaic blue of the sky. Feuer frei! We catapult three-sixty. We grenade, gravel, and stone the snowy fields below.

We shoot at vanishing points.

And then, as we were going hoarse and, desperate for a worthy cause, readying to disembowel each other, my little sis and I, there was—no other way to say it—there was something like an apparition.

Come from who knows where, cause we hadn't seen anything pass on that road since we'd taken up our positions that morning: a sudden monster, stark black against the blinding white.

Like a tree. A walking tree. We discern the branches, a giant pile of branches swaying in rhythm.

But it's not a tree, it's a donkey, a beast of burden, crisscrossing the snow under the branches.

Except it's not a donkey either.

15.

Vestiges

It's an old woman, all hunchbacked, all dressed in black. So hunched under her bundle of twigs that it looks like she's walking on four legs.

She must be deaf because our gravel, our flatulent salvos, and our screams have no effect on her.

We watch her pass, swaying under a bundle of sticks bigger than her.

Bewildered, we are. Nailed to the spot, to the floor of our bastions, mouths shut. We cease fire. Mum.

We hide under our blankets until it's time to go look for more hay for our mother, who's arriving soon at the nearest train station. We know she gets cold easy. We don't want her to catch her death in our inheritance.

But this rustic tableau: our father, Poulette, and me, in that empty room, lit by a miserable little oil lamp, with the cooking pot boiling in the smoky fireplace, and with hay up to our ears, it disheartened her immediately, our poor little mother who's usually so valiant.

She said, Jérôme, you can't be serious . . . ! And then she abruptly collapsed into the hay and fell quiet.

Yup . . . Jérôme . . . I know, it's perplexing.

Everyone calls our father Philippe, or Phil for fun. Even the notary. Our mother, she calls him Jérôme, we don't know why. Sometimes she even calls him Daniel.

So truly, we have no clue.

Maybe his real name is something else altogether.

Same with Oberkampf.

Oberkampf, like the metro station. Cause that's where we got our name from, the metro station.

Our real name (the original, I mean) is lost.

You have to understand.

Our father, his family, they got lost. He lost them, or maybe they lost him. Jérôme-Daniel-Philippe Something. This was during one of those lurid debacles that seem to happen so often throughout History. But we don't know which debacle . . . There've been so many.

Getting lost amidst industrial horror, amidst the panic of hunted, hounded crowds fleeing, strafed all down the roads, over fields, in camps, fronts, frontiers, trenches, and entrenchments, these things naturally happen.

After which, naturally, our father washed up

in a penal colony where the homeland bred cannon fodder like calves or battery-cage chickens for the slaughterhouse.

Cause the homeland foresaw it might come in handsy . . .

Of course, we weren't going to have a redo of 1914. It works the first time: fanfare and all that jazz of martial and national delirium. The next time round there's no one left to go clear out the enemy trenches with a bayonet.

You had to anticipate, to forestall trouble on the edges of the Empire. For once you couldn't blame the Administration or accuse the top brass of klutziness. They had clearly suspected there would be gooks and ragheads to frag after they'd tasked them with raking up the Fritz. In case they took a liking to it. Gotta be prepared.

So the little paupers, the ones come from who knows where and maybe from nothing, the genealogy-less, the lost, it'd be charitable to herd them in lock-step onto the path of honor and glory. Who would mourn them? The homeland would suffer less. And they might well save said homeland's skin and even some face.

Which is why we have a metro station's name.

Which is why we live in the muddy brown, the beige, the khaki, the heinous hazel, in sum, in the fetid fetish color of the infantry troops, in the allegorical folds of the true banner of the foot soldier.

All our porcelain sanitary ware: camouflaged!

Our tiles: fit for service!

Our walls? Off-white, but so off you'd think they'd crushed an A-rab into it, like we were at a review of the 11th shock chute regiment.

The fall tones, the cadaveric lividities of the troop most desperately devoted to being chopped up, the universal camouflage of the rifleman who strings out his guts over fifty yards, wallows in carrion of friend, foe, whomever, and attempts to hide there, those were our colors.

If, after graduating from his original penal colony, our father had at least been chucked in the navy, or the air force . . . But airplanes, those are delicate machines! And the pilots too!

He might be airborne, he might be chuted, but the infantryman inevitably reverts to his atavistic schmear.

Still, we're perplexed, cause in the infantry, what does our father do? We don't know. Nurse? Mechanic? Unclear. Maybe a nurse-mechanic, like there are singer-songwriters and secretary-generals, even if secreting is obviously not the same as generalizing and these are two different professions.

So we don't know what our father got thrown into: engineering, logistics, nursing, marching band . . .

What's for sure is that wherever they chucked him, he was able to give free rein to his philentropic passion.

Beat-up meat, smashed machinery, our father can fix it all. In times of war, even just during drills, stuff gets fucked very quickly.

Think of everything we've invented to kill! As if we don't unhinge rapidly enough on our own . . . As if our croaking weren't already guaranteed . . . Everything we've invented to slay our poor puppets! All those ingenious refinements to accelerate the fatal process . . .

How little it takes to kick the nugget and give up the toast.

A wisp, a mote . . . A ratchet that can't hack it, cardialgia, nostalgia . . . Even old things that lie around unused, they can still kill us. So imagine, with all these muddern inventions on top of it . . .

We die of vestiges, we die of speed.

We're muddern. We're supersonic. And it's a tiny little untimely residue that breaks your heart when its violent rending strikes you down in midair . . .

The ligamentum arteriosum, I bet you don't even know what it is, bet you don't even know you have one. It's almost nothing, some mortal thing dating back to, back to . . . Dating back to even before you were born, back to your aquatic life. It's the traitorous vestige attached to your aorta that keeps it in place. And it's that little villainous ligament, which was formerly an artery, back when you were a shrimp, a tadpole, a toad, a fetus, that will cause your aorta to rupture at the first untimely and violent acceleration . . .

The most perplexifying perplexity is what our father does with his days. We've asked him.

"First you take care of 'em and then you kill 'em? Or else first you kill 'em and then you take care of 'em? And then you have to kill 'em again, or what?"

We don't know the order of operations. We can't figure it out. Too much contradictory information, too many redactions in the reports.

It's also possible that he kills 'em by taking care of 'em, or takes care of 'em by killing 'em. Which is the more heroic? The most pontificent?

History wrapped in a fiddle inside a guerrilla.

Our little mother, for example, we always make sure to scrupulously take care of her after we almost kill her. But this time, faced with our little Jesus manger, our chamber pots, and the bare floor of the slain Fagarotti's hovel, we feared a fatal blow had been struck and that our mother's ligamentum arteriosum might not hold out.

Cause with Papa's inheritance, we immediately regressed into the primitive. All that effort since the ancien régime, all that suffering, all that toil, all that painful scrimping, that ever renewed distress over a poor nest egg ripped apart by wars, nibbled away by governments, mended endlessly, mended without respite . . . and we'd lapsed back to being hicks stranded in straw, stuck in the sticks, once again in total peenury and without any muddern comforts.

16.

Of Wolves and Cannibals

FOR OUR FATHER, ON THE other gland, it was exciting.

Another hovel meant another chance to achieve optimal muddernization, down to the last detail. With our training, we'd improved. We were muddernizing faster and faster. With (we thought . . .) less and less collateral damage and fewer incidental leaks. It was a more and more convincing muddernity. Maybe one day our sites might even be stylish . . .

We put our little mother back on the train toot sweet.

We remained in rearguard to take advantage of the fresh mountain air a little longer.

Poulette and I, we don't lower our guard. We replenish the cannonball stash. We helmet ourselves with chamber pots. We perfect our fortifications. We shore up our curtain walls, double down on our surrounding bastions.

We play cards with Mr. Koala under the blankets. But we're bored stiff in our icy garrison. Neuroses, psychoses, perversions, and other civil frivolities can only entertain for so long.

We yearn for bloodier distractions.

We require more heroic horrors.

So we play Russian roulette. We cock our Colts.

We pretend we're risking a bullet to the noggin. We try to imagine what it'd really feel like, to pull the trigger and go kaput.

We get drunk off the delicious odor of flint and plucked chicken skin flambéed in black powder. And since we've got nothing better to do than blow our brains out for fun, by nightfall, after so many fuses detonated against our temples, we're almost deaf.

It's the last day.

We've had it up to our eyeballs with slopes and peaks.

So we plan an assault on our own citadel.

We'll capture it in a historic surge, a stunningly suicidal furia francese.

With no artillery preparation.

With no preliminary sapping.

Without having starved the garrison through a customary siege.

We stampede our glacis. We scale our bluffs on hands and knees. We thrash about like demons in stoups of frost. We rush all the defenses. We take bastion after bastion.

We massacre entire garrisons of Saracens and Brits with grenades and bayonets.

We do it all, Poulette and I. We fall on our swords. We rush violently from the tops of the ramparts. We rise up from the bottoms of pits and relaunch the assault.

We lose and recapture the fort twenty times. Douaumont! Namur! Atrociously devastated, we fall over and over. We annihilate ourselves.

And then we demolish: we open savage breaches in the curtain walls with powerful whacks of the shovel and the pitchfork. We raze our bunkers.

We bury ourselves under the ruins.

It's the last, it's the great, it's the fateful dusk.

So we resurrect ourselves one last time to resume the struggle in a frantic surge.

Our citadel is fucked. We're drenched in sweat, Angélique and I, knocked back onto our rubble. To the east, the crests are tinged with a sad, sinister pink. Everything is turning to gray around us. Soon the cold swallowing up the valley will crash down on our hides and petrify our marrows.

We scrutinize the far peaks growing dark, one last time.

Then, and only then, did we notice.

In the sky to our right, the plume of smoke that

rises each day from the chimney of the house at the foot of the slope—where'd it go? And why're the blinds closed?

We went with our father, we knocked right on the door, storm lantern in hand, cause by the time we'd sounded the alarm, the call to arms, drummed wildly and gathered the squadron, it was dark as inside an oven between the village walls.

We knock for so long and so forcefully that the door mysteriously opens on its own.

Inside, it's as dark as in our own hovel. The only difference is the bundles of sticks piled from floor to ceiling.

A similar loft ladder leads to an identically dark room with an equally bare floor. Black fireplace, ashes, alcove, armoire, bitter cold. And in the bed, under the covers, a shriveled form.

In the fetal position.

A marionette, stiff and frozen. Beyond dead. Irreparable.

So we climb back down the loft ladder. We go home and bunk and bury ourselves again in the nice warm hay in our house, the fruitcake's former house. Our father says when we leave tomorrow, we'll stop at the gendarmerie to give a report.

That night, in the hay, in my head, I can't think of anything to tweak or wax or buff. But I can't sleep either. I swear I hear wolves outside, prowling around and talking to each other.

There's also an owl nearby going HOOT HOOT HOOT.

Poulette and the pater would later insist it was merely the wind that'd picked up and was blowing hard, sweeping our chimney duct.

But they don't know what they're talking about.

They were snoring loud enough to wake the dead while I was counting sheep and strands of hay under the covers protecting me from the cold and the moths, wondering what we'd do in the morning if we couldn't start the rustbucket, if it was out of gas.

Would we set out on foot in the snowdrifts, the cold, and the wind?

Have to be wary. What with the precedent of the Russian retreat, which was not a wild success. And what's more, if we got lost, if we strayed from the path and wandered into forgotten valleys and reached the real end of the world, we'd never see our mother again.

Or would we stay put and wait for help?

I try to take stock of our provisions, how many cans of corned beef, sardines, and soup we have left. But without the koala, it's impossible to know. My tablets aren't up to date and I don't dare get up to check, or even to take an incidental leak in my chamber pot.

If help takes a while to reach us, on account of the

storm, or a signal box error, and hunger starts tormenting us, will we turn into cannibals?

And if we turned into cannibals, what would be better? To eat? To sacrifice yourself? To fight fiercely to avoid being devoured by your ascendants, your descendants, your kin?

We'll draw straws, of course. That's how it's done in the best navies, on the occasion of the most pitiful shipwrecks.

But whom would I rather eat?

Poulette would be tenderer, but there'd be much less to eat. Our father, though tough, would last us longer. Maybe if we rationed ourselves he could last us until help arrived, or at least until the thaw, the breaking of the ice, and the spring.

But what if Poulette and the pater get it into their heads to sink their teeth into me? What if they decide to roast me or turn me into a ragout . . . ?

Wouldn't I rather we take our chances braving the cold and the snowy roads to try to make it back to civilization? If the alternative is ending up a stew, it'd be better for all three of us to be hounded by wolves and devoured by Cossacks.

That'd be jollier.

And maybe we'd stand a chance of capturing one, a Cossack or a wolf, and then we could have a feast around a campfire.

Still, I can't figure whether it's more humane and less cruel to eat your family or friends than to take a bite out of strangers.

I try to imagine it. I make a drumstick of each in my head, and I consider the first bite. I chew it mentally and study its effect on me, whether it activates my salivary or lachrymal glands.

I'll never know what's more humane, cause I must've fallen asleep chewing the Cossack around a nice campfire after our father got us lost in the snowy nocturnal immensity of the end of the world.

In the morning, the rustbucket started up glandily, so we'll also never know if we would've become cannibals.

But even if the rustbucket'd been out of commission, and we hadn't been able to resuscitate it, I think our father would've surely done what he always does. He would've left, wading all alone through the ocean of snow in search of help, abandoning me and Poulette in the hovel at the end of the world, or in the meager bivouac in no man's gland with the crumbs of a Cossack fit only to be thrown to the wolves.

And we would've waited for him on the hay or in the snow, like we're waiting for him now, in the sticks, in concrete.

HOOT HOOT HOOT goes the owl way out in the Styx, at the edge, at the end of a world.

And I'm still here, my two feet in my untroweled layer of concrete, next to Poulette snoring in her sarcophagus. And I think our father, who left yesterday saying Don't move, children, I'll be back . . . Well, we're still waiting for him so either he's forgotten us, or he's out of gas again.

17.

Dashing Gnashers

ANGÉLIQUE WAS SLEEPING, SHELTERED IN her sarcophagus. She was snoring, even.

Me, unarmored, uncasketed, I was telling stories to stay awake. I was telling stories more for myself, to stave off the solitude and horror of the night, when I saw the wall opposite me turn pink, pink like the tongue of a panting pooch, a pink of unprecedented softness.

I step out of my shoes, I go to the door, and from there I see the sunrise, and silhouetted against the morning twilight I see, all hunched over in her uphill trek, my grandma, cape tied around her shoulders, cane and lantern in her hand.

Oh joy!

I ran to her, in my socks on the pebbles.

She'd waited all evening for us to come back, and, when she couldn't wait any longer, she'd taken off in the night, leaving Grandpa at the house in case we reappeared.

She'd walked all night, not getting lost despite the darkness, despite the farmland consolidations that scrambled the landmarks and multiplied the dead-end paths.

She's old, so she can't run, but she walks resolutely. She stops sometimes midhill to catch her breath, when her heart grows tired, races and torments her. Then she starts again.

Wars, mourning, sorrows, horrors, she knows, she's seen them all. Nothing scares her anymore. Not even the solitude and night on the old roads, familiar and strange.

She's come to save us.

So we go adagietto rubato, amidst the aromas of dew and trampled grass along the road, Grandma pulling the washboiler on its scrap of wood, me pushing it, Angélique inside, still crystallized in her concrete.

I feel such happiness after such a dark night, after the intense fear and despair of waiting, that I start to sing.

I sing that the river is deep and if you wanted to, we could sleep together in a big square bed and we'd be happy until the end of the world.

Suddenly, out from a hedge in front of us pops a scarecrow in bloody rags, crowned with barbed wire and trailed by a magnificent Charolais bull whose majestic and grotesque balls skim the grass along the road.

Staggering apparition, petrifying vision . . . the kind that rips out your aorta and slam-dunks your heart into your shorts.

It took us some time to recognize him, but it was our father, who'd toiled all night in the stampedes and cut a rug through meadows, woods, fields, thickets, and pastures.

Don't move, children! I'll be back . . . and our pater had heil-tailed it. He'd taken a bumpy shortcut and broken down far from all civilization, all traffic. All the more so cause the shortcut was a big detour.

Now, he didn't break down cause he ran out of gas. He suffered a total engine breakdown. Our father could have tried pissing in the crack of the engine block, I don't think it would have moved anything. At best a burst of steam out of the cylinder head's ear . . .

He would have had better luck blowing smoke up the ass of a corpse.

So our father, cut off from all civilization, decided to cut through meadows and fields to reach home faster.

He cut so courageously that he got lost and delayed.

It wasn't that he'd forgotten about us, course not.

It was that night fell while our father was galloping through the pastures.

The moon, the famous moon for which I'd so

longed, turned the night blue, populating the pastures with pale ghosts, their pallor like a premonition, an indescribable horror.

Phantoms of large white motionless cows, lying swaddled in blankets of fog creeping out of humid valleys.

Our father was flayed already from scaling fences and weaving through hedges and thickets, but he didn't have time to suffer or wallow in the terror of the cows' spectral whiteness.

He roamed. He galloped. He got lost.

And then he realized he wasn't the only one galloping.

Turning around, he caught a glimpse of the triple quintal of meat and horns hot on his trail.

And that's why, in the moonlight, with a beastie on his ass, galloping panickedly through the pastures, our father didn't see the fence. Otherwise, certainly, he would've jumped or hedgehopped or hedgehogged like in a live-ammo drill.

But our father crashed into the fence at breakneck speed. He ran into it at full throttle. And there he hung, trussed like a turkey, frantically tangled in four rows of barbed wire . . .

He awaited the fatal goring. He was already picturing his guts uncoiling over fifty yards, like a good foot soldier. He was already imagining the color of his viscera in the light of the full moon when the bull stopped short just before him.

It mooed.

And it started to lick his wounds.

At first, our father thought it was a case of iron deficiency, or a lack of salt or various other minerals, and that once the beast had munched his rug it'd start to munch on his bones to extract his marrow.

He was wildly mistaken, our father.

The bull had been a calf. And the calf had a story.

THE STORY OF THE CALF

We have an old aunt. Maybe even a great-aunt. Her husband is one-legged. We call him the wobbler. They have a son.

The husband of an aunt, according to our mother, is an uncle (by marriage).

The husband of an aunt, according to our father, is an auntie.

Except this one in particular, the husband of this aunt, is no auntie. He's decorated, and not for Socratizing the deputy prefects but for having volunteered one day, a long time ago, to clean out a trench with his bayonet.

Seems to me, though I've never cleaned out a trench with a bayonet (I tried in my head, but it's not at all convincing, none of my glands budge . . . I really do try, but it bewilders me, full stop), that such a cleaning method would probably make everything filthier. Maybe with a pitchfork, I could see it . . . but nabbing the Krauts with the end of a bayonet and hoisting them like bales of hay onto wagons?!

The wobbler, the scour-Kraut artist, maidservant of the trenches, is a little old man, ancient and shriveled, who falls off his rocker when he's had more than two drinks and yells obscenities when his bottle's confiscated.

Our father also explains that if our aunt had the balls, we'd call her uncle.

So, between the uncles who are aunties and those who aren't, and the aunts who have balls and are called uncle, I get confused.

When I ask Poulette, clever as she is, to explain all these genealogical matters, to spell it out for me, she says, Let sleeping dogs lie . . .

I'm happy to let dogs sleep. To each his bone. But why would they lie?

She won't say.

Hysterectomy wrapped in piddle inside smegma.

They're funny ones, aunties.

There's a general who sometimes comes to dinner at our house. We always receive him with the greatest ceremony, this General Kraft or Graft, and he'll pontificate politely for hours with our father.

He's decorated like a Christmas tree. He has the biggest medal from the Legion of Honor Poulette and I have ever seen, and also dashing gnashers. So dashing that we wonder if he stole his dentures from a mule or kept the jaw of his deceased girlfriend, a flirty English motorized nurse, and had them stuffed so he could wear them himself, in her memory.

And so Gratz or Grentz, with his formidable chompers, often speaks of a woman we've never met, a certain Eugénie, who must be the wife of an uncle Eugène. One of General Quartz's uncles. Cause, although we have an uncle Gene on our mother's side, he's not married. So unmarried that we worry he'll bequeef us even more ruined and unsellable hovels and swaths of moorland that we wouldn't recognize even if we were stepping in them.

Monsieur Kroitz or Kreutz, in any case, gets along famously with this unknown-to-the-battalion Auntie Gene or Jenny. He's always talking about hooking people up with said Gen or Jenna later, and this makes him laugh.

Angélique asked him who this woman was whose horn he was tooting. Apparently she has something to do with the electrical company. Or with chuting.

The famous Gen or Jenna, suffice it to say we've never seen hide nor hair of her.

Maybe they're in a fight, she and Mr. Krauatz.

Or maybe she's a widow and lives as a recluse.

Maybe they hide her cause she's an embarrassment to the family.

Who knows? Krankz laughs and opens his fangs wide.

We'll never know.

Trickery wrapped in spittle inside a militia.

I'm not the only one who can't remember the name of mister formidable chompers. Our father, to keep things simple, when he speaks of him in his absence, simply calls him the Butcher.

Why the Butcher?

Our father doesn't want to say, and we're expressly forbidden to utter this word when Kroutz or Klutz comes to dinner.

So we don't know.

But I'm getting off topic, imagine that . . .

Not too far off. I promised you the calf and here we are talking about the Butcher. Isn't that usually where calves end up?

And anyway, if I digress, it's only to better reach the ending. I learned that from our father. He's always trying to find shortcuts, and he hurries, gallops, and gets lost. So I do the opposite.

Ergo.

The son of the one-legged guy who's not an aunt and of the aunt who doesn't have balls (otherwise we'd call her uncle) is our cousin. Maybe even a great-cousin. He raises oxen and collects porcelain sanitary ware.

They live in epic filth. The wobbler, ever since he finished cleaning out the trenches, must have developed an allergy to sweeping. To get from the kitchen to the barn, you have to trudge through excrement.

Which is paradoxical, given how many toilet bowls they have at their disposal.

When you take a piss at their house, it's not just one toilet bowl crowding the closet, not even just two. Instead of a WC they should call it a quadruple-UC.

It's the most beautiful collection of muck in the district, maybe even the universe. Cracked bidets, crusty toilets: this is what brings happiness and prosperity to our lame great-cousins.

They imagine themselves sitting atop treasure, thinking their old shitters, their antique thrones, are worth a fortune on the secondhand market. They're suspicious of the plumber who comes to change a sink or a leaky faucet, they accuse him of ripping them off, swindling them, robbing them if he even hints at making off with the broken piece.

They flatter themselves thinking they can resell everything at a profit.

That somewhere the secondhand shitter market is booming.

Maybe on that mysterious muddern thing they call the ouèbe.

Let's start the bidding: barely worn bathtubs, decayed toilet bowls where grateful cheeks have unleashed and rinsed, in high demand all over the world, from the bourgeois townhouses of the subprefecture all the way to Cacablanca.

The wares overflow into the garden, the barns, the cellars. They're in the attic and under the beds. They're under the stairs and on top of the beasties' troughs.

Our reserve corps, by comparison, seems meager.

Now, the wobbler's son has the highest regard for our father's philentropic vocation. When we're in the vicinity he no longer calls the vet for the big beasties. He consults our father.

So we visit the stable often. We wade in the swamps of liquid manure. We sink in up to our knees. Afterwards, our shoes are hazardous waste. We leave our pants at the dry cleaner and then we don't dare set foot there again.

Which is how our father found himself giving complimentary care to a handicapped calf.

It started with bovine physical therapy. Our father thought rehabilitation would suffice to spare the calf from the slaughterhouse or, worse, the butcher. Cause he wasn't suffering from a congenital malformation, just a bad dislocation, possibly the result of a rushed birth.

To make sure he wouldn't end up at the butcher's, our father even bought the calf from the wobbler's son. But he couldn't go to the stable to care for him every day. Soon he'd have nothing left to wear, shoes or pants. So we moved the calf in with us.

Our father had planned to have him climb into our sedan. He'd measured the calf and the back seat, but he was worried about aggravating the calf's dislocation. So our cousin lifted the animal, strapped into a belly-band, onto a hay trailer. He raised the barriers on each side, and same thing upon our arrival: hoist, strap, gentle deposit onto the grass.

No stress, no trauma.

The calf spent the summer there. Relaxing, ruminating. His eyelashes and gaze so soft. His horns peeking out from under the swirls of soft fur on his forehead. His warm, sweet odor. So sweet that I'd nap near him in the afternoon and we'd converse.

Our father bent the calf's leg for fifteen straight minutes, morning, noon, and night. He massaged it. He gave him water. He bottle-fed him vitamins.

After a week, we helped our father lift the calf so he could walk. We propped up our Charolais, helped him with his first shaky steps. Angélique on one side, me on the other, and our father pushing his butt.

Have to assume the rehabilitation had worked wonders for the calf. Cause it was the same calf, now a magnificent bull, who'd thrown himself into frenzied pursuit of our father, who'd broken into a panicked gallop through the dark prairies the day of the concrete . . .

He had recognized him, the calf, our father.

18.

Unmolding

OUR PROCESSION THROUGH THE VILLAGE—Grandma, Poulette, me, our father, and his bull—caused a sensation.

We stuck out like sore thumbs.

The washboiler shuddering on its scrap of oak and its wheels, the gravel ringing in it.

The gray petrified kid stuck inside.

The triple quintal of Charolais, nuts swinging from side to side through the daisies, meekly shadowing a limping man camouflaged in bits of mud and dried blood.

And then all the mutts in unison, a true honor guard.

Cause it's not only the calves our father looks after.

The dogs, the scraggly ones chained up in the ruins of chicken coops under corrugated iron roofs, the ferocious ones that sleep outside, the flea-ridden ones emit a concert of howls when we leave the countryside at the end of the summer. They know, they sense, when our carriage approaches, that the time of the family's great migration has come. There is universal canine mourning throughout the village.

So imagine our triumphant entrance!

They seem ferocious, but it's only because they've been deprived of affection. The proof: when our father gets out of the car and goes towards the foaming beast it jumps with joy and licks him clean with grateful slobber.

When we set out on our big returns to the city, we stop in front of every farm so our father can personally shake the pooches' paws and receive their blessings.

So's not to vex the farmers by stopping only for their mongrels, we force ourselves to say our hellos. This obliges Grandma and Grandpa to perform greetings they'd rather avoid. Grandma isn't from this village and Grandpa doesn't much care for company. He says only the morons were left behind and only the meanest came home. All the others are dead.

He still visits an old lady he knew in grade school. He knew her before she was an old lady. Apparently she was even a little girl back then. She always gives us an exquisite black-currant syrup while she chats with our grandpa.

She must have been a delicious little girl.

I dearly wish I had known this old lady when she was a little girl. But it was so long ago. I'd have to dive so deep and swim so hard against the current of time . . .

For a long time I would dream of plunging headfirst against the current of time, turning back its course to the moment when I could have known the exquisite little girl and her black-currant syrup, and also, with a bit of luck, I could have known my beloved grandma as she appears in the photo smiling at me with her clogs on the wrong feet.

I try in my head, at night. But the river's deep . . .

The house of the little girl with the black-currant syrup is at the very top of the village; it's the most beautiful view you can imagine, elevated, above the wooded hills and ridges. Like you could take flight without ever falling back down to earth.

We never leave her house without an old Manufrance catalog that she saves just for us.

A thrilling read I take with me to the bathroom.

We recently acquired a septic tank, but I still use the wooden john under the shed so I can get some pees and quiet. Amidst the odor of cut hay and buzzing flies, I devour pages and pages.

Hardware—what a marvel . . .

I run through entire lists at night after lights-out in my bed. I sort all of it with delight. I sort it before it all ends up in a jumble, before entropy swallows and devours us.

Why does everything in our house always end up in a monstrous jumble? I often ask myself.

At the start of his life, our father was poor. He had nothing. Barely a pot to piss in. Not even a hankie. And then, suddenly, a corn of copia . . .

Adonai how much.

It made him feel rich. But at the same time, he was completely overwhelmed. He didn't know where to put it all. He'd never had the schooling, the training . . .

When it comes to managing their affairs, their proliferating trinkets, their plethoric porcelain, the rich inherit the necessary techniques along with the merchandise. Not him. And chuting is no substitute.

Hens the mess . . . As the calf is my witness!!!

There was bric-a-brac everywhere. So much splayed inside, it was deluxe luxurious luxury. We wanted for nothing. We'd never want for anything again. Until the end of time. Until the final resurrection of all the waste, all the carcasses, all the vestiges.

But an apocalypse with no system is just a guaranteed scatastrophe.

You have only to watch our father in action to understand the last two centuries of France's military disasters, our grandpa declares. Berezina, Sedan, Bazeilles, the Marne, Verdun, and all those wars lost because of battles won in a magnificent surge and all those lamentable triumphs.

All those debacles, those victories that bleed and exhaust us.

Our bones piled up in sinister necropoles.

And mud and boards and tinkering—ingenious!—with shovel and pitchfork, and feet in mortar made from blood, shit, human carrion and vile vanity while the Fritz hose you down from their concrete bunkers with their clean socks, their feet nice and dry, from within the comfort of electricity, the nests of machine guns, the Saxony porcelain, crossfire and hot soup galore.

Our grandpa is a methodical civilian. You could even say he's extremely civil. Always, all the time. Methodically. Not servile. Civil. Service, be it military or domestic—that's the start of servility. That's what turns civilians servile and makes them lose all civility.

Which is why our grandpa meticulously shines his own shoes and why he didn't want to remain a foot soldier after the war even though his successive commanders tried to keep him.

He's very calm amidst this muddernization unleashed.

From time to time he goes to examine the wreckage, the collateral damage.

Our father offered to customize his radio: increased

power, patch to the record player, a huge antenna for better reception . . .

He refused.

He explained to us: heedless improvements, preferential treatments, wild stampedes, you have to be wary. In '17 they offered to transfer him to a quiet front. He boarded a ship: goodbye hell and hello Dardanelles.

He said he preferred not to.

If you're going to die for France, might as well die in situ.

He's the one, naturally, whom we entrust with missions requiring care, precision . . .

The unmolding and restoration of Poulette took him all day. Our grandpa got to work methodically, with nutcrackers, toothbrushes, tweezers, and an exfoliating glove.

Meanwhile, our father was spinning in circles in the courtyard, peering from behind the windows to see how it was going, seeking opportunities to electrifry himself once and for all.

Later we'll dismantle the hoist to conduct a postmortar: blasted gasket.

Later we'll repatriate the concrete mixer: paralyzed in a concrete coating.

Later our father's little toe, you know, the one the sledgehammer landed on, we'll ampootate it for good.

Later we'll establish, by consulting the koala and redoing our inventory, that our father'd decided, to speed things up and cause we were a little short on cement, to make those last drums with quick-setting concrete mix.

Hens why Angélique was statufied semi-instantaneously.

Hens also why the last concrete drum started to harden so rapidly.

Hens the supermechanical effort of the concrete mixer.

Hens the overheating of the engine and the circuit and the fatal paralysis.

Later, when the wobbler's son tows our rustbucket into the courtyard and we examine it head to toe, we'll notice that the cap of the plughole, under the crankcase, was screwed back in crooked after our father'd siphoned the oil needed to anoint the hoist, and that the bumps from the shortcut had gradually dislodged it.

Hens the massive oil leakage along the road.

Hens the motor heating and hiccuping and jamming and then completely paralyzing, a pilgrimage to Lourdes its only hope.

For once it wasn't the gas . . . But the mishap, the terrible viscosity of the mishap.

It's only a bladder of time till you're foiled by oil. And I don't even know anymore which is worse: to be on empty or to be full.

Mishap, I said.

Hens the stampede.

Hens the unexpected consequences of all our adventures.

Hens hurtling into the first breach that presents itself, without thinking twice.

Hens new and unexpected mishaps and their proliferation among the ingenious and complicated inventions cobbled together haphazardly and the centrifugal surge of vicious cycles.

Which wring us dry, wipe us out.

When all our time is taken up with setbacks, when setbacks are all we have left, when we only hurtle against the current of history, the more we advance, the more we recede.

Our father, not only is he entropy, but on top of that he's James Brown, he's Michael Jackson: the more he rushes forward, the more he slips back.

But it's not just the fear of time that runs through you, that carries and displaces and leads you astray.

The world engulfs you too.

Last winter the old woman who lives by the river had a stroke. One of her nephews dumped her in the county hospice, a place you only leave feetfirst. That is, if they haven't already ampootated those feet of yours to spare you from gaseous gangrene and to keep you from galloping through the hallways after lights out as you try to escape and piss off the paltry night staff.

When we returned to the countryside, when we took up our summer residence, we found in our rusty mailbox a page ripped from a notebook, which had probably been soaked several times before drying and redrying. On it was a note in waterlogged ink, a note from our Lady saying she doesn't know where they'll place her, that she hopes to see us again, that she'll be sure to come back when she can, one summer, to find us.

We entrusted the letter, signed Catherine Legrand, to the koala.

At night, in my head, I think of her, and I wonder where they placed our Lady and how we'll ever find her again. If they didn't lose her, if she didn't get lost. Even in prison. Especially in prison.

And it hits me all at once, the idea that the world is enormously big, that we get lost in it and that we're so easily displaced I wouldn't even know where to begin if I wanted to find Catherine Legrand again.

Where would I look?

We wanted to relaunch the war in her honor. But we were lacking enemies. We made an effort, Angélique and I, to find some.

In the space of a year, the kids in the village had either gone soft, or they'd become wary of us.

We went around on our bikes inviting the kids from the next village over to a rumble. We even provoked them.

Poulette called then names.

Brits, dicks, Fritz, baby bovines, and bearded brotula.

Vermifuge strumpets, limping pigeons, bumbling beavers, flannel willies, puny unicorns, shrill cat bowels, and symphonic gonads.

Bald monkeys, fluted rug rats, gleaming trepidations, Norwegian omelets, pheasant creeps, snot of hairless turkeys, dumb as dirt, and slow as snails.

But they were either lacking in vocabulary or our reputation preceded us, and they didn't take the bait.

After the incident, we didn't do any more construction. We gave up muddernizing altogether. We settled for maintenance.

And the concrete mixer, what became of the concrete mixer?

Busted spooling; had to change the engine. We had a perfect one, an engine originally belonging to the washing machine (the famous original washing machine).

It wasn't a standard swap. It gave the concrete mixer a wild increase in speed. But that didn't cure its Parkinson's. We ballasted it and bound it, but every time we plug it in it leaps and drags its ball of chains and cinder blocks up and down the courtyard.

Picture St. Vitus's dance.

It's no longer a concrete mixer, or maybe it's a concrete mixer-upper, a giga-mortar-flicker, an automatic cement render that we should really patent.

Beware! Do not stand in front of it, otherwise it'll lambaste you and stuff your mug full of gravelly spittle.

Have to aim the mouth of the drum at a wall, and then it's impeccable: it thoroughly pebble-dashes a full twenty yards in the space of a single wool-and-delicates cycle.

If you're in a rush, it can do the same thing five times faster on the spin cycle at two thousand r.p.m.

But first we had to scour the rapid-dry concrete that had crusted over the concrete mixer's walls, inside the drum and outside and all over, from the legs to the ring gear.

So while Grandma and Grandpa were unmolding Poulette, our father was unmolding the concrete mixer with a big rock.

"What about the sledgehammer," you might ask, "where's the sledgehammer when you need it?"

That we never found out.

The koala was tongue-fried.

Cliturgy wrapped in a diddle inside a chinchilla.

A Note from the Translator

Translating Anne Garréta's *In Concrete* is like trying to catch an eel in one pond and put it in another. Every time I think I have it in my sights, have lured it over, grabbed hold of it, it wriggles out of my hands with glee and dashes ever further away.

Or maybe it's like being in a batting cage with baseballs flying at my face and I have no bat and no helmet.

Or maybe it's like being in shark-infested waters and realizing, suddenly, that there's no cage around me.

Or maybe it's like reaching my hand into a bag, groping for my keys, but the bag keeps going and going, my hand grazes nothing, my keys are nowhere to be found.

Or maybe it's like throwing a rock into a well and never hearing the little crash as it collides with the bottom.

In Concrete is a novel, but it's also a fable, a feminist inversion of a domestic drama, somewhere between nursery rhyme and Oulipian text—Zazie in the Concrete if Zazie had gone to the École Normale Supérieure. Garréta invents her own novel form, blurring the boundary between spoken and written language, showing the wild mutability and playfulness of language as its own machine of modernization, acting out on the page how the words spoken around us infiltrate our own ways of speaking and understanding systems of language. How does the racism or homophobia of those around us insinuate itself into our speech? How do the thought patterns of our parents find their way into our vocabulary? Perhaps the trickiest part of translating *In Concrete* was capturing the narrator's voice, because it is in fact a multiplicity of voices: a language bath.

Anne and I spoke about the book after she'd read my translation of the first two chapters. My notes from that conversation say: "Sex puns. Shit puns." "Go *à fond*. Go whole hog." "Get drunk and see if we get good puns."

Every paragraph of this book, and sometimes every sentence within a given paragraph, contains some kind of obstacle to overcome, its construction slowly crumbling to pieces when analyzed beyond face value. When something in my translation seemed off, as though I had missed a reference, often I would ask Anne for clarity, only to watch an entire sentence, paragraph, page unravel before my eyes as the layers upon layers of semantic meaning lurking beneath the surface became clear and I was faced with the task of starting from scratch to make sure all of it was brought into the English text as well.

In Concrete is, above all, an exploration of language. There's the narrator's homophonic language, which is not as well suited to English as it is to French, as misspellings can be more inventive and playful in French without being mistaken for text or online speak. There are the technical terms about building sites, concrete mixers, electrical conduits, and various plumbing systems. There are the references to war, to French idioms, to European culture. There are sexual innuendos, scatological innuendos, and homoerotic innuendos that might not be interpreted the same way for an American audience as for a French audience. There is the juxtaposition between the voice of the young, 12-year-old narrator, and their precocious, outlandish, or even unbelievable knowledge of history and vocabulary.

Most painfully and most satisfyingly, there are the plays on words. The never-ending plays on words. The infinitely expanding and interlooping plays on words. The plays on words that span entire paragraphs or entire chapters, that work across English and French and sometimes even German, because Anne Garréta is able to take for granted that her readers will have a cursory knowledge of all three. Plays on words that hinge on a particular unit of the French language, or ripple through several sounds of French words, or depend on a certain subset of regional or historical knowledge.

Anne Garréta's wordplay delights in turning French inside out, using its sounds and spellings and the multiple meanings of its words to make her readers laugh, make them revel in their everyday language and see it in a new light. Because French and English are different languages, because English sounds and spellings are not as easily toyed with, because the double meanings of an English word do not always match up with the double meaning of the word Garréta has chosen to use in a specific instance, because what makes a French reader laugh might not be what makes an American reader laugh, because of these reasons and more, my translation differs in many ways from Garréta's original.

To keep Garréta's homophonic language from coming across in English as slang, as text speak, or as an imitation of a regional accent, my solution was to use it only in places where it couldn't be confused for any of those things. For example, phrases such as "may swell begin at the beginning," "too mush rushing around," "it snot a good time," "punkchewation," and more. I also relied heavily on linguistic blurriness, like the sliding from concrete to 'crete to up shit's 'crete, from the sticks to the Styx, or the gray area between what a kid might hear and what they might think they hear, such as words like "muddernization," "electrifried," "bequeef," "scatastrophe," and so on and so fork.

Because I lost some of the wonderful, childlike homophonic language and slippery syntax of the French, I strove to use more alliteration ("assassinated ass-bandit"), more excessive apostrophes ("Who'd've thought?"), more childish verbifying of words ("we'd concrete every weekend in the countryside"), and cute, comprehensible but unusual ways of using language ("reswooned" and "rechewed").

I also employed more callbacks, more pilings on to earlier puns, upping the ante with each new iteration of the joke. In Garréta's French text, there is a play on the word *glandu*. The narrator is in awe of the inner workings of the body, specifically the many glands and their various functions. The narrator remarks that "l'humain est drôlement glandu." This is understood in context to mean that humans are chock full of glands, but *glandu* is also a word used to describe someone stupid. Because I lost this specific play on words in English, I found other ways to pun with the word gland throughout the text—there's glandsformation, there's glandemonium, the father has too much time on his glands. One missed wordplay turned into an opportunity for a proliferation of puns.

My tactic was to exploit the places where English had room for linguistic play as often as I could, absorbing each sentence and contorting it in my head to see if there was room for a joke. For example, the concrete mixer engine dies by shuffling off its mortar coil, and subsequently the father must perform a postmortar. Declining machines bite the rust. The grandmother is the guardian of proper grammar and syntax in the narrator's life, and when the narrator's spelling starts to slip, there is a purposeful ambiguity between who or what is suffering: it is simply the gramma. I exploited words like "wading" for waiting, "hens" for hence, and "handsy" for handy. Phrases like lickety-spit and yestergear. And I was thrilled to have an opportunity to use the phrase "throw in the trowel," a pun uniquely suited for exactly this book.

I also wanted to harken to the French original by inserting French word plays where I could in my English translation ("we didn't have any time toulouse" or "we put our little mother back on the train toot sweet"). Sometimes it was as simple as using a word that made me laugh. I hope my use of the word "dingus" made readers laugh, as well.

I started this translation in a cozy room at the CITL translator's residency in Arles in the summer of 2019, battling a sinus infection and eating a lot of Frosted Flakes. I finished a first draft in the coldest winter days

I've ever known at the Banff Leighton Artist Studios in Canada in January 2020. In late August 2020, amidst a pandemic and a Providence heat wave, I sat sweating in my apartment during multiple Zoom calls with Anne Garréta as we fine-tuned the finished translation. Anne would ask whether I was stocked up on essentials in preparation for the next wave of the coronavirus, and took note of my birth date so she could send me a happy birthday email just a few days after I had turned in the translation. One day, on a Zoom call I expected would be our last, I came prepared with what I thought were a few simple follow up questions after reading over the full draft again, a handful of places where I realized I wasn't fully confident in what the text meant. But every question I asked opened up a new set of questions, revealed a reference or a pun that I hadn't yet unraveled, fueled more Zoom calls and more conversations.

As Anne explained the multiple layers contained within one particularly thorny phrase to do with electrical torture, watching as my face fell in the Zoom window, she apologized for subjecting me to a very different kind of torture with this translation. What I most savored during these calls were the moments of laughter, whether spurred by heat stroke or delirious desperation, and the triumph and cheer when at last we found a solution to a problem that had previously induced anguish.

Even when translating experimental, intricate texts whose wit and charm relies heavily on the mechanics of the language they were originally written in, there are always solutions in translation, there are always ways to bring the spirit, voice, sharpness, and hilarity of the author's text into a new language. But it requires calling on different methods, breaking different linguistic rules, inventing different comedic patterns, pulling ourselves back from the brink of defeat and finding new ways of peering into our own language to tease out all of its potential.

Emma Ramadan
Providence, September 2020

Anne F. Garréta is a graduate of the Ecole Normale Supérieure, received her License de Lettres at the Université Paris 4 (Sorbonne), her Maitrise and her D.E.A at the Université Paris 7 (Diderot), and a PhD at New York University. The author of six novels, Garréta was coopted to the Oulipo in 2000. Her first novel, *Sphinx* (1986), which caused a sensation when Deep Vellum published its first English translation in 2015, tells a love story between two people without giving any indication of grammatical gender for the narrator or their lover. She won France's prestigious Prix Médicis in 2002 and the Albertine Prize in 2018 for her book, *Not One Day*, which was also nominated for a Lambda Literary Award. Garréta teaches regularly in France at the Université Rennes 2, and more recently at Paris 7 (Diderot), and is a professor at Duke University.

Emma Ramadan is a literary translator of poetry and prose from France, the Middle East, and North Africa. She is the recipient of a Fulbright, an NEA Translation Fellowship, a PEN/Heim grant, and the 2018 Albertine Prize. Her translations for Deep Vellum include Anne Garréta's *Sphinx* and *Not One Day*, Fouad Laroui's *The Curious Case of Dassoukine's Trousers*, and Brice Matthieussent's *Revenge of the Translator*. She is based in Providence, RI, where she co-owns Riffraff bookstore and bar.

The translator would like to thank Anne F. Garréta, Daniel Levin Becker, and Lucy Lavabre for their contributions to the translation.

PARTNERS

FIRST EDITION MEMBERSHIP
Anonymous (9)
Donna Wilhelm

TRANSLATOR'S CIRCLE
Ben & Sharon Fountain
Meriwether Evans

PRINTER'S PRESS MEMBERSHIP
Allred Capital Management
Robert Appel
Charles Dee Mitchell
Cullen Schaar
David Tomlinson & Kathryn Berry
Jeff Leuschel
Judy Pollock
Loretta Siciliano
Lori Feathers
Mary Ann Thompson-Frenk & Joshua Frenk
Matthew Rittmayer
Nick Storch
Pixel and Texel
Social Venture Partners Dallas
Stephen Bullock

AUTHOR'S LEAGUE
Christie Tull
Farley Houston
Jacob Seifring
Lissa Dunlay
Stephen Bullock
Steven Kornajcik
Thomas DiPiero

PUBLISHER'S LEAGUE
Adam Rekerdres
Christie Tull
Justin Childress
Kay Cattarulla
KMGMT
Olga Kislova

EDITOR'S LEAGUE
Amrit Dhir
Brandon Kennedy
Dallas Sonnier
Garth Hallberg
Greg McConeghy
Linda Nell Evans
Mary Moore Grimaldi
Mike Kaminsky
Patricia Storace
Ryan Todd
Steven Harding
Suejean Kim
Symphonic Source
Wendy Belcher

READER'S LEAGUE
Caitlin Baker
Caroline Casey
Carolyn Mulligan
Chilton Thomson
Cody Cosmic & Jeremy Hays
Jeff Waxman
Joseph Milazzo
Kayla Finstein
Kelly Britson
Kelly & Corby Baxter
Marian Schwartz & Reid Minot
Marlo D. Cruz Pagan
Maryam Baig
Peggy Carr
Susan Ernst

ADDITIONAL DONORS
Alan Shockley
Amanda & Bjorn Beer
Andrew Yorke
Anonymous (10)
Anthony Messenger
Ashley Milne Shadoin
Bob & Katherine Penn
Brandon Childress
Charley Mitcherson
Charley Rejsek
Cheryl Thompson
Chloe Pak
Cone Johnson
CS Maynard
Daniel J. Hale
Daniela Hurezanu
Dori Boone-Costantino
Ed Nawotka
Elizabeth Gillette
Erin Kubatzky
Ester & Matt Harrison
Grace Kenney
Hillary Richards
JJ Italiano
Jeremy Hughes
John Darnielle
Julie Janicke Muhsmann
Kelly Falconer
Laura Thomson
Lea Courington
Leigh Ann Pike
Lowell Frye
Maaza Mengiste

pixel texel

ADDITIONAL DONORS, CONT'D

Mark Haber
Mary Cline
Maynard Thomson
Michael Reklis
Mike Soto
Mokhtar Ramadan
Nikki & Dennis Gibson
Patrick Kukucka
Patrick Kutcher
Rev. Elizabeth & Neil Moseley
Richard Meyer
Scott & Katy Nimmons
Sherry Perry
Sydneyann Binion
Stephen Harding
Stephen Williamson
Susan Carp
Susan Ernst
Theater Jones
Tim Perttula
Tony Thomson

SUBSCRIBERS

Ned Russin
Michael Binkley
Michael Schneiderman
Aviya Kushner
Kenneth McClain
Eugenie Cha
Stephen Fuller
Joseph Rebella
Brian Matthew Kim
Anthony Brown
Michael Lighty
Erin Kubatzky
Shelby Vincent
Margaret Terwey
Ben Fountain

MARIA GABRIELA LLANSOL · *The Geography of Rebels Trilogy: The Book of Communities; The Remaining Life; In the House of July & August*
translated by Audrey Young · PORTUGAL

PABLO MARTÍN SÁNCHEZ · *The Anarchist Who Shared My Name*
translated by Jeff Diteman · SPAIN

DOROTA MASŁOWSKA · *Honey, I Killed the Cats*
translated by Benjamin Paloff · POLAND

BRICE MATTHIEUSSENT· *Revenge of the Translator*
translated by Emma Ramadan · FRANCE

LINA MERUANE · *Seeing Red*
translated by Megan McDowell · CHILE

VALÉRIE MRÉJEN · *Black Forest*
translated by Katie Shireen Assef · FRANCE

FISTON MWANZA MUJILA · *Tram 83*
translated by Roland Glasser · DEMOCRATIC REPUBLIC OF CONGO

GORAN PETROVIĆ · *At the Lucky Hand, aka The Sixty-Nine Drawers*
translated by Peter Agnone · SERBIA

ILJA LEONARD PFEIJFFER · *La Superba*
translated by Michele Hutchison · NETHERLANDS

RICARDO PIGLIA · *Target in the Night*
translated by Sergio Waisman · ARGENTINA

SERGIO PITOL · *The Art of Flight* · *The Journey* · *The Magician of Vienna* · *Mephisto's Waltz: Selected Short Stories*
translated by George Henson · MEXICO

EDUARDO RABASA · *A Zero-Sum Game*
translated by Christina MacSweeney · MEXICO

ZAHIA RAHMANI · *"Muslim": A Novel*
translated by Matthew Reeck · FRANCE/ALGERIA

JUAN RULFO · *The Golden Cockerel & Other Writings*
translated by Douglas J. Weatherford · MEXICO

OLEG SENTSOV · *Life Went On Anyway*
translated by Uilleam Blacker · UKRAINE

MIKHAIL SHISHKIN · *Calligraphy Lesson: The Collected Stories*
translated by Marian Schwartz, Leo Shtutin, Mariya Bashkatova, Sylvia Maizell · RUSSIA

ÓFEIGUR SIGURÐSSON · *Öræfi: The Wasteland*
translated by Lytton Smith · ICELAND

MUSTAFA STITOU · *Two Half Faces*
translated by David Colmer · NETHERLANDS

FORTHCOMING FROM DEEP VELLUM

MAGDA CARNECI · *FEM*
translated by Sean Cotter · ROMANIA

MIRCEA CĂRTĂRESCU · *Solenoid*
translated by Sean Cotter · ROMANIA

MATHILDE CLARK · *Lone Star*
translated by Martin Aitken · DENMARK

LOGEN CURE · *Welcome to Midland: Poems* · USA

PETER DIMOCK · *Daybook from Sheep Meadow* · USA

CLAUDIA ULLOA DONOSO · *Little Bird*, translated by Lily Meyer · PERU/NORWAY

LEYLÂ ERBIL · *A Strange Woman*
translated by Nermin Menemencioğlu · TURKEY

ROSS FARRAR · *Ross Sings Cheree & the Animated Dark: Poems* · USA

FERNANDA GARCIA LAU · *Out of the Cage*
translated by Will Vanderhyden · ARGENTINA

ANNE GARRÉTA · *In/concrete*
translated by Emma Ramadan · FRANCE

JUNG YOUNG MOON · *Arriving in a Thick Fog*
translated by Mah Eunji and Jeffrey Karvonen · SOUTH KOREA

FISTON MWANZA MUJILA · *The Villain's Dance*, translated by Roland Glasser · *The River in the Belly: Selected Poems*, translated by Bret Maney · DEMOCRATIC REPUBLIC OF CONGO

LUDMILLA PETRUSHEVSKAYA · *Kidnapped: A Crime Story*, translated by Marian Schwartz · *The New Adventures of Helen: Magical Tales*, translated by Jane Bugaeva · RUSSIA

JULIE POOLE · *Bright Specimen: Poems from the Texas Herbarium* · USA

MANON STEFAN ROS · *The Blue Book of Nebo* · WALES

ETHAN RUTHERFORD · *Farthest South & Other Stories* · USA

BOB TRAMMELL · *The Origins of the Avant-Garde in Dallas & Other Stories* · USA